BISCAYNE INFERNO

and Other Stories

BISCAYNE
INFERNO
and Other Stories

Oscar Fuentes
"The Biscayne Poet"

Jitney Books

#MADEINDADE
#MIAMIFULLTIME

For my parents, who crossed their own infernos so I could write mine.

BISCAYNE INFERNO
and Other Stories

TABLE OF CONTENTS

Biscayne Inferno

Chapter One: Body Furnace

It happened late one night right after my friends left my room at the Vagabond Hotel. I had just gone down for a nap. I was almost falling asleep when someone knocked on the door. Someone knocked three times.

I thought, *Whoever it is, they're going to have to knock six times for me to get up from this cozy bed and answer that door.*

The more this person knocked repeatedly, the more I tried to guess who was behind that door. I had no clue. Finally, the six knocks were about to cue my answering.

I took a deep breath and screamed from my Cadillac bed, "WHO IS IT?"

Then I heard a woman's voice. "Open the fucking door, Oscar!"

I couldn't recognize the voice. I got worried. I got off the bed immediately, put my ear against the door, and I was able to hear another voice whispering. That's when the door exploded and knocked me down to the ground. I hit my head so hard against the wooden floor that my world went black. I don't know if I was out for a minute or an hour.

When I woke up, I had a pounding pain on the back of my head. I tried to get up, but someone had nailed my pants and shirt onto the Vagabond's Florida pine wood floor. I couldn't move at all. My vision was blurry; I couldn't see the faces that surrounded me clearly. Then I heard the voice of a man.

"Do you want me to chop him up into little pieces, Chacha? Huh? Huh?"

"Beads, calm the fuck down. We just want to scare him, not kill him! Give me the knife and the gun," said Chacha.

"What are you gonna do to him, Chacha? Are you gonna chop him up into little pieces? Huh? Huh?" said Beads.

"Beads! You're annoying the fuck out of me! Get the fuck out of here and go wait for me in the car!"

Somehow, I felt safer without that guy named Beads around. With his exit, the woman closed the door of my apartment and locked it.

She walked over to me, bent over to face me and said, "I know you're wondering about who we are and why we are doing this to you. It's all very simple, Oscar. We just want you to hand over the Mayan artifact your grandfather gave you. Just give me the artifact and we'll be gone before you know it."

I was so confused, wondering, *How did they know I carried the artifact my grandfather had given me? How did they even know about it?*

Then Beads came back into the room.

"Is he talking yet? Did you search the room?"

"Not yet. He's all yours," she said pointing at me, as if giving him permission to do something.

Chacha went to the closet and started looking and searching through my clothes and dresser drawers.

Meanwhile, Beads stood over me, looking deep into my eyes. He was a short bald muscular man with no teeth. His mouth was opened, wrinkled lips hanging, big jaws and tattoos covering his arms. His face was covered in pimples and small blisters. It dawned on me that he had a Russian accent.

I looked at him and said, "You're a strange looking dude..."

"What did you say, mudderfukker?"

"That you're a strange looking fellow, you fuck head!" I responded with an anger that came from a disarming fear of dying without fighting for my life.

He threw himself at me and hit my face with his forehead. My nose was bloody and broken.

"I'm a strange looking dude, huh?" he countered while slapping my face hard, but I couldn't feel anything.

My face was numb with a constant shock of pain.

He kept on asking and repeating, "I'm a strange looking dude? I'm a strange looking dude? I'm a strange looking dude? I'm a strange looking dude? Huh? Huh?"

He took hold of a hammer and started removing the nails from the wooden floor. I could feel my shirt and pants loosening from the floor. He kept on repeating the question. I could feel the blood from my nose running down the back of my throat. I was breathing through my mouth. I didn't say anything else to him. I wanted to make sure I was completely loose.

He was fast with the hammer, and while he continued to concentrate on his morbid mantra, I searched the room with my blurry vision and spotted Chacha sitting on my bed. She had found my Mayan artifact. She held it with her right hand and dialed a number using my cellphone with her left.

Then she turned to him and said, "Take him to the bathtub and take off his clothes."

Beads, the mutant, got quiet, grabbed my arms, dragged me all the way to the bathtub, and threw me in there.

I could hear Chacha talking with someone on the phone, but couldn't make out what she was saying.

Beads turned on the hot water and forgot to turn on the cold. I didn't even have the strength to open my eyes. I could feel the hot water burning my skin, and I started waking up slowly from the pain on my face.

I wanted to scream, but I couldn't. Chacha came over and started unbuttoning my bloody shirt and pants. I laid there in my boxers, burning under the steamy hot water, feeling more awake. They both stood there watching me.

I noticed she pulled out my artifact from her right pant pocket and gave it to Beads.

"Take this to Tony G. He's waiting for you at Van Orsdel," she said.

He turned to go, but she grabbed him from his elbow and pulled him in close, "If you lose this, Tony will incinerate us both."

He looked at her with his frozen, crazy eyes and said, "I won't fucking lose it. Now let go of my fucking arm."

Beads exited the bathroom, then the room. Chacha leaned toward me to turn off the hot water. That's when I grabbed her fast by her shoulders and pulled her hard toward me as I rammed my bloody forehead against her face.

Then blackout.

The next thing I remember is waking up with her limp body over me. I had knocked us both out. I was able to push her off of me with the little strength I had left. I could feel my face pulsating.

I crawled out of the bloody tub and pulled my weak body up with the bathroom sink counter. I looked at myself in the mirror. My nose looked five times larger with the swelling.

Chapter Two: Biscayne Inferno

The mirror in the Vagabond gave me back a stranger's face. Nose swollen. Eye bruised. I didn't care. The thugs who had come to assault me at the hotel would be surprised to see me alive.

The hammer and knife lay on the floor. I wrapped them in a motel towel and grabbed my car keys and phone. My '74 Dodge Dart waited outside with its trunk full of old typewriters—ghost keys possessed by the spirits of hundreds of dead writers who had once owned them until their middle fingers got stuck from a severe case of Dupuytren's Contracture.

I left the Vagabond in a hurry, heading south on Biscayne toward Van Orsdel Crematorium. The Mayan artifact my grandfather gave me on his deathbed needed recovering. I had to retrieve it before it disappeared forever.

The Dart coughed, then roared awake. I pressed the gas. It leapt forward like the devil on a leash, every gear shift a tug at the chain. I almost let it go.

Somewhere between the neon of pawn shops and the crematory sign, I saw her: Amara Li. First in a dream days ago, and now, in a flash vision from the future.

She sat beside me on the bench seat, translucent and barefoot, dress wet, hair slick as if combed by the tide. She looked ahead, not at me.

The city broke in a pause.

The present dissolved. I was underwater. Biscayne Boulevard was a drowned causeway. Condos like reefs, balconies heavy with coral. Street signs swayed, unreadable. Cemeteries emptied. My own ashes dissolved in saltwater, drifting in the Biscayne currents. It hit me like a tsunami I didn't see coming, salt and decay, fear and awe so murky I could not breathe.

Her hand brushed the rearview mirror.

"You've been here before," she said.

Her voice was a current through time. I gripped the wheel for control. I could feel her presence, the future spilling into the present. The hammer and knife hummed.

My grandfather's dying words echoed: *You are its keeper. Its voice is yours.*

The Dart tore down Biscayne Boulevard, southbound. Typewriters clattered in the trunk, like ghost fingers on keys. The city rose and fell around me, living and drowning. The air smelled of salt and something else I couldn't name.

I didn't understand it, but I didn't need to. The artifact, the flood, the ghost beside me, they were all the same. I was moving through time—through an undertow—and I was moving fast.

I made a right on Biscayne and Northeast 34th Street. The Dart stopped in front of Van Orsdel Crematorium, engine ticking down, headlights spilling across cracked pavement.

I pushed the door open and got out. My shirt was bloody, boxers torn. I had the knife in one hand, the hammer in the other.

Above the crematorium, the sky had turned unnatural—burgundy and red streaked with blue and purple. Lightning flashed slow and deliberate, like the heartbeat of some enormous, unseen storm. A category seven hurricane seemed trapped in the clouds, waiting.

I knew the artifact was inside. Activated. Calling me. I could feel its pulse through the metal in my hands, through the blood on my skin, through the heat of the smoky air.

The wind carried the smell of ash, ozone, and salt. I didn't look back at the Dart. The typewriters rattled in the trunk like a warning, ghost keys clicking in the dark.

The door was cracked open, and smoke poured out in thick, black waves. The smell, faintly barbecue. I stepped inside. My lungs started to burn.

The crematorium was a furnace. Flames roared along the walls, devouring everything. The furnaces were abandoned. Bodies lay still beneath the smoke and heat, untouched.

The artifact burned in the back center of the room, white-hot, red-hot, almost alive. I could feel it throbbing in my hands before I even touched it.

Something glimmered on the floor—a single heat-resistant glove. I dropped the hammer with a loud thud and snatched it, palm slick with sweat, fingers stinging from the heat.

Then the artifact was in my gloved hand.

The smoke clawed at my throat. I stumbled forward. Amara was inside my mind, her presence warm and urgent, threading through memories of that Miami night when the AC had broken and she had first whispered into my dreams: *It tests you. Not for strength. For everything you are.*

I moved down the center aisle, past rows of marble niches, blackened urns, and stainless-steel beds on wheels, every step slow. Shadows clung to the walls, but I could see enough to keep my footing. Lightning from the storm above streaked through stained-glass windows, casting long stripes of burgundy, violet, and blue across the floor. The artifact pulsed in response, a steady rhythm I could follow in the dark.

At the far end, Amara waited, hovering just above the ground, hair slick, eyes reflecting the storm outside.

She did not speak aloud, but I heard her voice in my head: *Do not falter. You are its keeper.*

Smoke curled around the edges but did not obscure the way. I stepped forward, knife steady in one hand, hot artifact in the other, following the exit door light.

The artifact pulsed harder, demanding, insistent, alive. I could feel it threading through me, through everything I was, everything I had ever thrived for. I remembered my grandfather.

I moved back toward the exit, lungs burning, smoke thickening enough to remind me of the danger, but not so much I couldn't see the path.

That's when I saw them.

Two bodies sprawled on the floor, semi-fresh but already catching flame. The stench hit me first—sickly sweet, mixed with scorched leather. The fire crawled up their clothes, licking at blistered skin, erasing faces I had last seen snarling in the half-light of my apartment. A flash, Beads on top of me, pulling the nails from the floor, and Chacha stealing the artifact. Another, the metallic taste of blood in my mouth as the door slammed behind them.

Now, their eyes—what was left—stared glassy into the dark, frozen wide as if they had seen what was coming but were too late to run. The flames made quick work, turning muscle to shadow, shadow to ash.

I stepped past without slowing, the artifact pulsing like a second heartbeat in my hand and made my way toward the exit.

Outside, Biscayne Boulevard sparkled with water. The Sinbad Motel at 62nd was half-submerged, its neon sign flickering, reflecting in shallow pools. The Dart waited, engine still growling, typewriters still rattling in the trunk. I climbed in, chest burning, muscles screaming. The artifact no longer burned hot but glowed beside me on the bench seat.

Amara Li whispered in my mind: *Alive. Wild-eyed. Burned but unbroken.*

I pressed the gas and headed back to the Vagabond Hotel. The city rushed past, alive, drowned, chaotic. I moved faster than the world could follow, the artifact glowing beside me. In the rearview mirror, everything slid away. I caught a glimpse of my strange, bloody face. And in that madness, I smiled.

Chapter Three: Airboat Escape to Vizcaya Mansion

Months later. I woke up in Room 116 at the Vagabond Hotel. My window faced the pool, though I couldn't see much. The floodwater had turned murky, a thick mix of green and brown, streaked with mud and debris. I imagined the tiled mermaids frozen underwater somewhere beneath the muck, mouths open like they were whispering secrets I couldn't hear.

The hotel was full of survivors from the northern flood: bankers with damp suits, thieves with wet wallets, lawyers, artists, librarians, musicians, school principals, Republicans, Democrats, Independents. the undecided. We all huddled around a made-shift bar at the edge of the balcony, sipping coffee that tasted like cardboard and too many long nights. Most of us were quiet. Some cried in silence. Some murmured, deciding where to go next.

The first floor was underwater. Everyone who'd stayed there now doubled up on the second floor, sharing rooms. I knew no one, and no one knocked on my door asking for shelter.

I looked out the back window. My new airboat rested in the flooded lot behind the hotel. I had traded the '74 Dodge Dart for it with a Jamaican-Honduran rum-smuggling friend named Jackson. He had wild eyes, teeth sharpened like sharks, and he swore the Dart could carry a full barrel of rum faster than any Coast Guard Patrol.

I had decided. The Vagabond Hotel was a cage of anxious, obnoxious survivors who had no idea how to survive. I was leaving it for good.

Vizcaya Mansion was my destination. Built on a high limestone ridge and surrounded by walls tall enough to hold back the flood, it had survived mostly unscathed. It was a hunch, a calculated effort, a promise to myself that I could find some order in chaos.

I climbed into the airboat. The engine roared to life: a Chevy LS V8, raw and unrelenting. Like a devil on a leash, it screamed over the floodwaters, vibrating the hull, throwing spray across my chest. The city behind me dissolved into silver chaos, half-submerged rooftops and flickering neon swallowed in water.

As I maneuvered the airboat through the bay, I could see debris tangled under the mangrove branches, furniture pieces, street signs, fragments of homes. Garbage floated in clusters, clinging to tree roots. They were reminders of the flood's mighty strength, the unstoppable force that had swallowed the city and killed or displaced more than ninety percent of Florida's population.

I pushed off, heading south along Biscayne Bay. The airboat cut through the water like a single-engine airplane, churning and splashing. The mermaids below—imagined somewhere under the muck—frozen in their endless swim.

Before I reached Vizcaya, I cut the engine. Silence fell, except for the drip of water from the mangroves. I paddled toward a small hiding spot, wedging the boat in roots, camouflaged with leaves and a green tarp. The LS V8 had a hidden surprise: a mounted shotgun—Jackson's gift, Florida-grade for hunting pythons.

I pressed myself against the mangroves, chest-deep in black water, leaves brushing my face. From the shadows, I could see the Vizcaya Mansion looming above, silent and perfect, but it wasn't empty.

Voices drifted through the heavy air, muffled but sharp enough to pierce the quiet.

"You shouldn't have killed that man," one voice snapped.

"He wasn't innocent!" another barked back.

"Put that gun away. We can't keep doing this!"

I froze, the words burning into my chest.

Another voice hissed low, urgent: "When we find a way out of here, we're gone. We're running out of food, water...everything."

Armed strangers. I could hear the steel in their words, the menace underneath. If they saw me—or even suspected I was here—they wouldn't just attack. They'd take the boat, and I'd be left stranded in the floodwaters, helpless. Everyone in the city had become a thief to survive. Everyone was fair game.

I waited, counting their words like heartbeats, then slid silently back through the roots, wading chest-deep to the hidden boat. Every step was careful, deliberate, avoiding sticks, roots, anything that might betray me.

Once I reached it, I pushed off slowly, still under cover of the mangroves, paddling far enough from the shore that I could safely start the engine without drawing attention. The LS V8 roared to life, slicing through the water like a hurricane propeller, churning silver waves southbound.

Biscayne Bay stretched ahead, open and wild, but I didn't look back. My eyes were on the horizon, searching for the Barnacle House in Coconut Grove. Somewhere safe, somewhere dry, somewhere I could breathe without listening for voices plotting in the shadows.

It was still early morning, only a few months after the flood had begun. I had the entire day ahead of me, every hour a negotiation: survive without getting killed, survive without having the boat stolen from me, survive without letting the city's new rules—every man for himself, every thief fair game—catch me unprepared.

The floodwaters shimmered in the pale light, restless and endless. The wind whipped my hair, cold and alive, and I felt the weight of a city that no longer existed, a world I could barely imagine beyond the horizon. The mermaids in my memory watched, somewhere under mud and muck, mouths open in silent warning. They were witnesses to a chaos I had no control over.

I had no word from the outside—no radio waves, no cell signal, no TV broadcasts. I didn't know the state of the country, the fate of the world. And yet, here I was, afloat, moving. Hands steady on the wheel, I let the airboat cut through the water, southbound through the remnants of a drowned city. I was alive in this moment—aware of the gloom, but carrying a thread of stubborn hope—moving fast, moving quiet, moving forward.

Chapter Four: Barnacle House—Nightfall Reflections

Night had settled thick over Biscayne Bay. I crouched by a fire, stick in hand, flames flickering against the dark water. The airboat was hidden, camouflaged beneath mangrove branches—a small island of safety in a world turned upside down. I had water heating in a small pot inside the Barnacle House. Scraps of food waited for me. I could survive tonight. I could survive tomorrow. But surviving wasn't enough anymore.

I need to go back north, I thought, watching sparks spiral into the night. *I need to see if my son and daughters are still out there. If they're alive. I need to try to bring them here, to the Barnacle, or at least know that I tried.*

The memory of my life before the flood came in fragments, jagged and bright. A family, a wife I had once kissed in the morning sun, the little hands of my daughters slipping into mine. Laughter echoing in the rooms of a home that no longer exists. I had been a husband, a father, a man with a life built of ordinary things. Now those ordinary things were gone, swallowed by water and fire and human desperation.

If they're alive, they're out there somewhere. And if they're not...then I'll know I tried. That I didn't leave it to chance. That I didn't wait too long.

I scanned the water, the mangroves, the horizon. Every sound was amplified—the drip of water from the eaves, the rustle of leaves, the distant crash of debris against the half-submerged streets. My hands flexed over the stick, over the wheel of the boat, over the world I could barely hold together.

I needed a radio. A walkie-talkie. Something that could catch a signal, a fragment of the outside world, some transmission to tell me that the world beyond the flood still breathed. Some voice that could tell me someone was alive, somewhere north, somewhere beyond Miami's drowned streets.

I can survive this. I have to survive this. And when I do...I'll find them. I'll find my children. I'll find a place that isn't drowning. I'll make it safe, even if I have to fight the entire world to do it.

The fire glowed against my face, shadows stretching long across the water. I felt the loneliness, the weight of months after the flood, more than ninety percent of Florida's population gone, but I also felt a spark of stubborn purpose, a thread tying me to hope, however fragile.

Tonight, I survive. Tonight, I plan. Tomorrow, I move north. Tomorrow, I search. And one day, if I am lucky, I bring them back here. To the Barnacle. To some small, quiet corner of this drowned world where we can be together, alive.

I rose, gathering the last sticks. The pot simmered softly. My eyes scanned the windows and doors. I moved deliberately, carefully, securing the Barnacle House. Locks clicked. Shutters banged into place. The airboat remained hidden, silent in the mangroves.

The night pressed in, dark and wet, but inside me, a pulse of determination thrummed. I was alive. And I would keep moving. I would keep surviving. I would return here with my children if I could. This would be our safe house. This would be the one place in the flood that could hold our world together, even if the rest of Florida had drowned.

Chapter Five: First Day at the Barnacle

The morning came gray and heavy. The wind moved the water like it was breathing. I had slept little. The fire had burned down to coals, and the pot of water was lukewarm. I drank some. My hands shook. Hunger and cold had the same taste.

The Barnacle House was quiet. I moved slowly, checking the locks again. Every window. Every door. The wood creaked, but it held. The flood had spared this hill—this small rise—just enough. I ran my fingers over the old wood, counting nails, counting screws, counting the days since the water took the city.

Outside, Coconut Grove was a graveyard. Pools of water reflected broken roofs and twisted cars. The smell of rot was strong. I exclusively breathed through my mouth. The street was empty. I looked for anything that moved for food—or for survival, or for something darker, a threat—but nothing. I walked down the narrow path between the Barnacle and the main road. Shadows of abandoned people flickered in memory only, and I moved past them. Gun over my shoulder, every noise mattered.

I found the small store once familiar, the corner of Coconut Grove where I used to walk past and see kids laughing. Looted. Shelves emptied. Floor wet. Broken glass was everywhere. I stopped in the doorway, imagining a younger me, hosting an open mic with Elizabeth and Mitchell. The memory stung. A reminder that life could exist here, once. Maybe it could again.

Back at the Barnacle, I needed a plan. I needed a way to know what was happening beyond the mangroves.

The radio in the kitchen was old, probably useless, but I needed it. Any static would be a message from the world, a thread I could pull. I rifled through cupboards. Dust and mold. A flashlight. A box of matches. I found a small transistor radio buried under old pots. I turned it on. Nothing. Only a hiss. I whispered curses into the dark. I needed to hear a voice. A hint. A signal.

Anything.

I started collecting wood. A fire outside, facing the bay, would cook what little I had and keep me warm. Stick in hand, I struck a match, careful not to waste it. Flames caught. I watched them lick the wood, alive and defiant. My hands trembled less now. My mind drifted.

I have to go north, I thought. *I need to see if my children are alive. Marcos. Camila. If they are, I'll bring them here. If not...I'll know I tried.*

The day stretched ahead, long and merciless. The sun tried to break through clouds, weak and gray. I could move fast in the airboat, but every turn, every canal, every shadow could hold someone desperate, armed, willing to kill for survival. The city had become a hunter's ground. Everyone was fair game. Everyone had learned the rules, or the lack of them.

I crouched beside the fire. The pot crackled. Smoke spiraled into the sky. I listened to it, imagining it could carry a message to my children, wherever they were. The radio still hissed. Static. Silence. The wind moved over the water.

I am alive, I told myself. *And that is enough for now. I will survive. I will find them. I will make this place safe for us. For whoever is left.*

The Barnacle House creaked in agreement. The windows reflected silver water. The mangroves whispered against the hull of the hidden airboat.

I could feel the day stretching before me, long and dangerous, full of opportunity and risk. I could not see the world beyond Biscayne Bay. I could not know if the country had survived. But here, in the murky water, among the debris, I could be alive. I could think. I could plan. And maybe, just maybe, I could bring a small part of the world back to life.

Chapter Six: Scavenger Day

I woke early. The Barnacle House was quiet. My hands itched to move. I had a plan: gather what I needed, prepare the boat, and head north. I had to know if my children were alive. Marcos. Camila. I had to try.

The air smelled of rot and water. Coconut Grove sprawled before me, streets flooded, debris everywhere. I ran my eyes over the pools and broken cars—the remnants of a city that had no rules anymore. Every movement could be dangerous. Everyone was a thief. Everyone could kill for a scrap.

I gathered my courage and started down the path. I needed supplies. Food. Water. Firewood. A working radio. Anything.

My mind kept ticking.

Stay quiet. Stay aware. Don't get distracted. Don't be seen.

I went first to an abandoned corner store. Shelves were empty. Broken glass crunched under my boots. I sifted through wet boxes. Rice. Canned beans. A rusty can opener. Good enough. I stuffed it in a bag I had scavenged the day before. I could cook with this. I could survive.

Next, I located what remained of the hardware store. Nails. Rope. Matches. A small cast iron pot. Perfect. My heart thumped, but I stayed calm. I ran my fingers over the items, imagining them in the Barnacle kitchen. I imagined the fire outside, the pot boiling, heat and smell of something real to eat.

The radio had to work. I found it hidden in a pile of ruined electronics. Old, scratched, but intact. I flicked the switch. Hiss. Silence. I cursed softly. Static was better than nothing. I could catch a voice. Someone alive. Someone telling me the world was still breathing.

I collected sticks and driftwood along the shoreline, everything small enough to carry. The wind moved the water. Trash floated past. Furniture, boards, plastic, broken chairs. A mattress or two, waterlogged, pressed against mangroves. I imagined the flood—strong, violent, unstoppable. It had taken almost everything. More than ninety percent of Florida's people were gone. Dead. Drowned. Killed by desperation.

By the time I returned to the Barnacle, the sun was high. The firepit waited. I arranged the wood. I checked the boat in the mangroves. Hidden. Camouflaged. Safe. For now. I ran my hand over the LS V8. It would carry me north. Fast. Quiet. Deadly if I needed it.

Inside the house, I set the small pot on the stove. Water boiled.

My mind ran. *I need to go north. I need to find them. I don't know if they're alive. I don't know if the world beyond Biscayne Bay still exists. But I will try. I have to.*

I packed the supplies into the boat. Rice, beans, water, pot, matches, ropes, the radio, the flashlight. I went over the plan again in my head. Quiet.

Fast. Avoid looters. Avoid anyone who could take the boat, shoot me, or worse. Every man for himself. Everyone is a thief. Everyone is fair game.

I looked at the Barnacle House. Windows. Doors. Locked. Secured. Safe.

This will be our safe house. I'll return. I'll bring them here if I can. I'll make it safe. I'll survive.

I glanced at the horizon. The sun reflected silver on the murky floodwater. My hands tightened on the wheel. I was ready. The boat hummed under the mangroves, patient, alive. I exhaled. One last look at the fire, at the house, at the water. Then I pushed off.

North. I was going north. To find them. To try. To survive. To bring some part of the world back from the flood.

Chapter Seven: Northbound Through the Drowned City

The day was still young. I had pushed off from the Barnacle, heading north through the murky canals, debris brushing the hull. The LS V8 thrummed beneath me, alive, impatient, a devil on a leash. I felt the wind in my hair, the smell of rot and salt. Everything was quiet, except for the water, the rustle of mangroves, and the distant calls of birds I didn't recognize anymore.

Then I saw them. Two boats—small, fast—cutting across the water like sharks. Thieves. Or scavengers. Or worse. I could hear the echo of gunfire already, faint but ominous. They had seen me. They wanted my airboat, my supplies, my life.

I tightened my grip, pressed my lips together and thought, *No. Not today. Not now. Not this.*

I pushed the throttle. The LS V8 roared. The airboat leapt over the water, spraying green-brown waves, the debris of a drowned city sticking to the hull. I looped around the first boat, then the second. Every turn precise, every motion calculated. They followed, slower, clumsier, guns raised, shooting into the spray behind me. Bullets hit the water with loud hisses, but I was already gone.

I held the shotgun. I didn't hesitate.

The barrels of my airboat were aimed at their engines. One shot. Sparks flew. Gas leaked into the air. Another shot. Flames caught. The first boat exploded into pieces, man and machine tossed into the sky.

The second boat tried to turn, tried to chase, but I circled them like a predator. Click. Empty. Not a shell left. But they didn't know that. They froze. Eyes wide. Guns raised. The air smelled of salt, smoke, and gasoline.

"Drop it," I said—my voice steady. Calm. Absolute.

They hesitated.

Then slowly, reluctantly, they lowered their weapons. Hands shaking. I could see the fear in their eyes. I grabbed the guns and ammunition they offered—two .45 caliber Glocks, a rifle with a telescopic sight, extra magazines, and a bundle of bullets. Enough to survive, enough to protect myself.

I stripped their extra gasoline from their boat and loaded it onto mine. They had no way to follow me now. I left them floating in the green-brown water, empty, stranded, powerless. My hand lingered on the wheel for a second. I could have done more. I could have punished them. But I didn't. I didn't have the heart. Not today.

The water shimmered beneath me. Debris floated past—broken furniture, pieces of a drowned city. Mangroves shook in the wind. The horizon stretched north. My children were out there. Somewhere. And I had survived this encounter. Had weapons, fuel, and the LS V8 beneath me. I could move. I could plan. I could live.

I leaned forward, scanning the water. The day long, full of danger, full of opportunity. I had no time to waste. North. Marcos. Victoria. Camila. Juni. Carmen. The Barnacle House waited. I would make it safe for them if I could.

The airboat roared to life again. I pushed it forward. Full speed. Every second counted.

Chapter Eight: Biscayne Park, Lost Paradise.

I arrived at my sunken neighborhood of Biscayne Park. Rooftops and houses were submerged in murky water. My old street stretched beneath me like a drowned memory. I shut off the airboat engine, stripped off my clothes, and dove in. Teeth chattering, my lungs braced for the cold.

I swam underwater toward the house I remembered, ducking past floating debris. Light filtered down in weak, distorted shafts. Broken furniture drifted like drowned ghosts. I found a shattered window and slipped inside, feeling the jagged edges scrape my hands. Inside, the water was darker, thicker. My fingers traced the walls, searching.

Then I found the height markings carved on the bathroom door frame. Nostalgia sank me. Sharp. Bitter. Sweet. Heavy.

And then, the photo. Confusion at first. Then, recognition. My children—older, unrecognizable—at milestones I had missed. Proof of a life I hadn't lived with them. My chest tightened. My vision blurred.

From the gloom, she appeared. Amara. She didn't swim. She coalesced like smoke—translucent and alien—swaying with a ghostly rhythm.

Her voice entered my skull directly, soft, intimate, terrifying.

You measure ghosts, Oscar Fuentes, she whispered in my mind. You search for a life you already lost.

Memories hit like waves. A door slamming. The sting of cheap paper as I wrote letters I never sent. My daughter's back retreating up the staircase, eyes full of disappointment. Chaotic. Unrelenting.

"No!" I gasped, bubbles escaping my lips. *This is a trick! They're out there! They need me!*

I pressed myself against the submerged ceiling of the house, barely breathing, cheek against cold plaster. The water pressed in all around me, my lungs burning. My eyes scanned the shadows.

Debris floated past. Broken furniture. Paper curling like dead leaves. I counted heartbeats. One. Two. Three.

A distant engine. Faint. Then, silence. Voices. Shouting. Men. Orders. Questions. I didn't answer, didn't move.

I touched the cold, slippery floorboards, shifted, and pressed tighter against the ceiling. Time slowed. The water moved with me. Every ripple was a warning. Every shadow was a threat.

I looked around. No one. Just murk. I pushed off the ceiling, swam underwater toward the broken window, and slipped out into the fresh air.

The sky was pale, distorted by the waves. The airboat waited.

Hands on the hull, my fingers were cold and trembling. I hauled myself in, my heart hammering, my mouth dry. I breathed fast.

I held my breath for an instant, and then, I heard them: men shouted, "There, I see him! Shoot!"

Then the engine roared. Reality hit. Gunshots. Bullets cutting the air.

I grabbed the shotgun, fired, ducked, and fired again. Two men charged from the water's edge. Both went down, their blood staining the murky water.

I noticed ripples moved beneath the sunken rooftops. Shadows stretched. And then, oversized alligators surged upward, eyes glinting, teeth glistening. They slid toward the floating bodies, feasting in the water red with blood.

I gunned the engine and paddled toward their abandoned craft. I scavenged guns, ammunition, and extra gasoline. My hands shook, heart still hammering.

The water trembled. They circled. Predators.

I put on my clothes over my wet body. I couldn't hear any other engines, but I sat in silence for a while longer. I saw flashes of the lush green neighborhood—Biscayne Park. Now, a lost paradise.

Chapter Nine: The Keeper's Pulse

The world had ended. Twice. Once for everyone else, in water and fire. And once for me, in a sunken living room, breathing from a pocket of air at the ceiling while a ghost told me the truth.

I don't know how long I drifted after the shooting. The sky turned from bruised purple to a flat, sickly gray. The airboat's engine was off, and the silence was a weight.

My hands wouldn't stop shaking.

It was a fine, constant tremor, the kind that starts deep in the bones after too much adrenaline and not enough hope. The image of that photo was burned onto the back of my eyes. My children, grown. Strangers.

Amara's words were a cold echo: *You measure ghosts, Oscar Fuentes.*

I was a ghost, haunting a drowned world where I'd already failed.

The cold seeped through my wet clothes. I fumbled in the damp pack, my numb fingers searching for a dry shirt, a half-pack of cigarettes, anything to ground me. I found neither. Instead, my fingers brushed against the rough, familiar texture of the artifact.

I flinched, expecting the searing heat of the crematorium.

But the heat was gone.

The artifact was warm. Not burning, not angry. Just a deep, gentle warmth, like a stone left in the sun. A soft, steady pulse beat against my palm—a slow, rhythmic thrum that vibrated up into my wrist. It was a heartbeat in the silence where my own felt weak and irregular.

I didn't pull it out. I was afraid of what I'd see. Afraid of Amara's face in the carving. I just held onto it in the dark—my knuckles white—clinging to its strange comfort like it was the only real thing left.

The shaking in my hands slowly subsided, syncing with the artifact's calm, insistent rhythm. I held onto it until the tremors stopped, until exhaustion pulled me down into a black, dreamless sleep.

I woke to a different world.

The first thing I noticed was the light. It was dawn, but a dawn filtered through a lens of impossible clarity. The second thing was the silence.

It was absolute.

I sat up, my body stiff and aching. And then, I froze.

The water was crystal clear. Not murky. Not green-brown with silt and decay. It was like looking through a pane of polished glass. The flood had always hidden its horrors, but now, it was revealing them with terrifying precision.

Twenty feet down, the submerged street was perfectly visible. I could see the yellow double line of the asphalt, a mailbox lying on its side, the skeleton of a car—its windows blown out. Sea grass swayed from a crack in the pavement, and schools of silver fish drifted lazily between the rooftops.

And then, I saw them.

Alligators. Maybe thirty of them. Of all sizes—from six-foot juveniles to monsters twelve feet long. They were moving in a wide, perfect circle at the bottom, their powerful tails swishing slowly, almost lazily. They weren't hunting. They weren't fighting. They moved with a slow, deliberate, hypnotic rhythm, like hands on a clock. Like a ritual.

They were circling directly beneath my airboat.

My breath caught in my throat. I should have been terrified. I should have been scrambling for the ignition, ready to scream the LS V8 to life and get the hell out of there. But a strange calm held me. They weren't looking up. They showed no interest in me. They swam as if they were asleep, trapped in a trance.

The artifact.

It was still in my hand, clutched against my chest. It was still warm, still pulsing with that same soft, steady rhythm. The rhythm of the circling gators.

You are its keeper. Its voice is yours.

The thought didn't feel like my own. It was just there, cold and certain. This was the artifact's doing. It had stilled the water. It had called them here. For what? Protection? Worship? I didn't know. The line between miracle and nightmare had dissolved.

As I watched the prehistoric circle below, the exhaustion and the artifact's warmth pulled me under again. My eyes grew heavy. The clear water, the circling monsters, it all became a lucid dream.

And then, the real dream began.

It wasn't a dream of the future. It was a memory. But not mine:

Water. Not clear, but churning, filthy, and rising fast. The view was low, a child's height. The sharp corner of a kitchen counter. A woman's hand—my ex-wife's hand—grabbing a can of food from a high shelf. Her face was tight with a fear I'd never seen before.

The sound of a generator sputtered, dying. A man's voice, not mine, never mine, yelled about the levees. Then, the view changed to a rain-lashed window. A military truck, olive green, rolled down the street. A soldier with a megaphone, his words eaten by the wind. But the meaning was clear: Evacuate. Now.

A small hand, Camila's hand? pointed. A sign on the truck, barely visible through the sheets of rain, read CONTINGENCY ROUTE 7 - HOMESTEAD A.F.S.

Then there was the feeling of being lifted. The world lurched. The window was replaced with the dark, crowded interior of the truck. The memory was a cocktail of terror and strange excitement. Then, nothing. A jolt. The sound of a gate closing. Not the end of the journey, but a pause.

The vision snapped off like a switched-off light.

I jerked awake, gasping.

The sun was higher. The water was still preternaturally clear. The alligators were still circling their silent, slow-motion carousel.

My heart was hammering, but not from fear.

From a terrible, burning clarity.

Homestead Air Force Station.

It wasn't a photo. It wasn't a ghost. It was a location. A place they were taken to. A place they might have been.

The artifact hadn't comforted me. It had tortured me with the truth, and then it had given me a clue. A grave. A starting line.

I wrapped the artifact carefully around my neck with a thin nylon string. Its pulse pressed warm against my chest, steady, insistent throughout the ride.

The artifact's pulse quickened in response, as if in agreement. I looked down at the circling guardians below and knew I wasn't alone. I had a devil on a leash, a ghost in my head, and an artifact that carried its own voice.

I fired up the LS V8. The roar shattered the sacred silence. The circle of alligators broke apart in a chaos of powerful tails and swirling sediment, fleeing the sudden noise.

I turned the boat south, toward Homestead, with the artifact's warmth and rhythm guiding me through the clear water and the unknown ahead.

Chapter Ten: Westward

The artifact's pulse was my compass, a steady thrum against my chest, pulling me south. The water—once again murky and choked with debris— seemed to part for me. I didn't question it. I just pushed the airboat, the LS V8 screaming its raw, mechanical prayer over the drowned world.

Homestead Air Force Base wasn't a base anymore. It was a fortress risen from the flood. Chain-link fences topped with razor wire encircled the higher ground, where hangars and administrative buildings stood like bleak islands. Military patrol boats, engines a low growl, cut through the waterways where runways used to be. The air smelled of diesel, boiled cabbage, and desperation.

I killed the engine a mile out, camouflaged the boat in a thicket of mangroves, and paddled the rest of the way in silence, my heart hammering a rhythm the artifact echoed back.

A soldier with a bored, sun-beaten face stopped me at a checkpoint.

"State your business."

"I'm looking for my family. Evacuees. They would have come in on Contingency Route 7."

He eyed my bloody shirt, my torn boxers, the wild look in my eyes. He saw a hundred of me a day.

"Processing is in Hangar C. Keep your hands where we can see 'em. No weapons inside."

Hangar C was a cavern of human misery. The air was thick with the smell of unwashed bodies and disinfectant. Cots stretched in endless rows. Families huddled together, their eyes hollow. I moved through the crowd, a ghost among ghosts, my eyes scanning for a familiar face, a laugh I'd recognize, a head of hair I used to ruffle.

"Marcos? Camila?" My voice was a dry croak, lost in the din.

Nothing.

I asked soldiers. I asked volunteers. I asked anyone who looked like they'd been there more than a week. I described them until my throat was raw. I got shrugs, pitying looks, and a single, chilling lead from a nurse changing a bandage.

"Route 7? They processed them fast. A lot of them were moved west weeks ago."

"West where?" I demanded, the artifact burning against my skin.

She shook her head, avoiding my eyes. "To make room. They said it was temporary. Krome. The old processing center. I don't know anything else."

Krome. The name was a tombstone in my gut.

A hand touched my elbow. I flinched, ready to fight.

It was a woman. Her eyes were the same shade of exhausted determination as mine. She wore a faded volunteer's vest, but it didn't fit her. Nothing here fit her.

"I heard you," she said, her voice low. "Asking about Krome."

"What do you know about it?"

"I know you don't want to go there looking like that," she said, her eyes flicking to my clothes, my desperation. "And I know I can't stay here another night. They're rationing bullets, not food. It's not safe."

She looked past me, toward the fences, the open water beyond.

"My name is Sol. I can get you past the patrols. I know the waterways. You get us out of here, and I take you to Krome. That's the deal."

It wasn't a request. It was a pact. I saw the steel in her. She wasn't just running from something; she was running toward something else. I nodded. No other words were needed.

We slipped out as the sun bled into the horizon, using a drainage culvert Sol knew was unguarded for a ten-minute window. We waded through muck to my hidden airboat. She didn't comment on the mounted shotgun, just nodded in approval.

I fired up the LS V8, its roar a declaration of war on the silence of the base behind us. We didn't speak. Sol took the front, her eyes reading the water like a map, pointing left or right with a sharp gesture to avoid submerged obstacles the flood had hidden.

West. We were going west. The artifact's pulse was a steady, approving drum against my chest. The sun vanished, leaving us in a twilight world of deep blue and black. The silhouettes of drowned houses stood like headstones. The world had become a continuous waterway, a graveyard of the past.

My stomach was a knot of hope and dread. Krome.

It was a direction. A purpose.

Sol's grip on the console tightened. "There," she whispered, pointing toward a cluster of rooftops jutting from the water at odd angles. A flooded neighborhood. "We should check. For supplies. For...anyone."

I cut the engine. The silence was heavier than the dark. We drifted. The only sound was the drip of water from the mangroves and the low, insistent hum of the artifact against my ribs.

I squinted at the water, searching for anything. An arm. A flash of color. A reflection that could be human.

And then I saw it.

A small figure clinging to a partially submerged fence, barely visible against the dark water. My pulse jumped. My family. Relief surged, but I forced it down. Panic could cost us everything now.

I called softly, my voice barely carrying over the water, "Hey! Over here!"

The figure's head turned. A face, pale and terrified, looked up. Recognition flickered in their eyes, fear melting into a fragile, desperate trust.

I paddled harder, closing the distance, careful not to tip the boat. Sol was already moving, leaning over the side, her hand outstretched.

For the first time in what felt like forever, we were reaching someone. Not safe yet. But together.

Chapter 11: The Sanctuary at Krome

The artifact pulsed against my chest. A slow, deep drumbeat. A warning. It knew before I did.

Krome wasn't a sanctuary. It was a scar on the face of the flood. A complex of low, brutalist buildings, once white, now streaked with waterline grime and rust. Chain-link fences topped with razor wire coiled into the brown water. Watchtowers made of splintered wood and corrugated metal stood crooked against the gray sky.

The air smelled of wet ash and shit.

A patrol boat found us before we got within two hundred yards. Two men. One young, eyes wide with a fear he tried to hide behind a rifle. The other, older, face like a worn-out boot. He held a shotgun loose in his hands. He didn't need to hide his fear. He was past it.

"That's far enough," Boot-Face said. His voice was gravel in a tin can. "State your business."

"We're looking for people," I said. My hand rested near the knife on my belt. "Family. Came in on Route 7."

He spat into the water.

"Everyone's looking for someone. What else you got?"

He eyed the airboat. Eyed Sol. His gaze was a physical touch. Dirty.

"We have fuel. Some food," Sol said, her voice steady, hard.

The young one's eyes flickered at that. Hunger. Boot-Face just smiled. No teeth. "You can bring it all inside. For a conversation with The Man. He decides what you keep."

It wasn't an offer. It was an order. The young one trained his rifle on us. A silent period to the sentence.

We motored slowly to a makeshift dock. They made us tie up. They made us empty our packs. Cans of beans. The rope. The water. Boot-Face picked up my knife. He weighed it in his hand. Smiled again. Slipped it in his own belt.

"For safekeeping," he said.

They took the glocks. The rifle. They left me the artifact. It hummed. Warm. Angry.

They marched us into the compound. People watched from doorways. Hollow faces. Eyes that had given up. A man missing a leg sat against a wall, staring at nothing. The smell got worse. Rot and piss and despair.

We were led to the largest building. Inside, it was dark. Candles flickered. The air was thick with smoke and the murmur of low voices.

At the far end, on a threadbare office chair, sat The Man.

He wasn't big. He was neat. His clothes were clean. His hair was combed. He looked like a school principal who had won a war. He held a plastic fork. He was eating something from a can. Beets. The juice was red, like blood on his lips.

Boot-Face shoved us forward. "Found 'em on the water. Asking about Route 7. Got a boat. Some supplies."

The Man looked up. His eyes were the coldest thing I'd ever seen. No emotion. Just calculation.

"Route 7 was a long time ago," he said. His voice was soft. You had to lean in to hear it. That was the trick. It made you lean in. "Names?"

"Fuentes," I said. "Marcos and Camila Fuentes. My children."

He took another bite of beet. Chewed slowly. Swallowed. "Children don't do well here. Too many mouths. Not enough food." He looked at Sol. "She's not their mother."

"No."

"What is she to you?"

I didn't answer. He smiled. A thin, blood-red line.

"You have a boat. That is a valuable thing. A thing that requires… contribution." He set the can down. "You can contribute. Everyone does."

That's when the screaming started.

Chapter 12: A Feast of Flies

The scream was high-pitched. Cut off with a wet gurgle.

It came from a side room. The door was ajar. The Man didn't even look. He watched me.

"A reminder of the price of greed," he said, so softly.

Boot-Face grinned. He walked to the door and kicked it open.

A man was on his knees. His face was a mask of blood. Another man stood over him, holding a tire iron. It was dripping. On the floor between them was a single, half-eaten can of peaches.

"Tried to hoard," The Man said. "The food belongs to everyone. The punishment belongs to everyone."

The man with the tire iron looked at The Man. The Man slightly nodded.

The tire iron went up. Came down. Not on the head. On the back. The sound was wrong. A thick, crunchy wetness. The man on the floor screamed again. A broken, airy sound.

The tire iron went up. Came down. Again. Again.

I couldn't look away. I saw every detail. The way the victim's body jolted. The specific way a rib cage gives. The spray of red mist on the boots of the man swinging the iron. The smell. Copper and shit. The flies. They were already there, buzzing around the pooling blood on the concrete.

Sol made a small sound. A choked-off gasp.

The Man heard it. He turned his cold eyes to her. "You find it unpleasant?"

She didn't answer. She was white. Shaking.

The swinging stopped. The only sound was heavy breathing from the man with the iron and a soft, mewling whimper from the thing on the floor.

The Man looked back at me. "Your contribution will be the boat. You will join our scavenging teams. You will be fed. She will be safe." He glanced at Leo, who was trembling, trying to be small. "The boy will be safe."

It was a lie. I could see the truth in his dead eyes. The boat was his. Sol would be his. The boy was leverage. I was a tool to be used and broken.

The artifact pulsed against my chest. A hot, insistent rhythm. Not a warning anymore. A command.

I looked at the ruined body on the floor.

I looked at the blood on the boots.

I nodded. "Okay."

The Man smiled his red smile. "Good. Welcome to Krome."

Chapter 13: The Deal Goes South

Night fell like a blanket. The compound settled into a tense, fearful quiet. The only lights were from The Man's building and the watchtowers.

We were given a corner of a room. A thin blanket. No food. No water. Our payment for contribution.

"We can't stay," Sol whispered.

Her voice was thin, like it might break if she said more. The fear wasn't just in her words, but in the way her hands twisted the corner of the blanket, the way her eyes flicked to the door every few seconds. She wasn't only scared of The Man or his guards. She was scared of what we were becoming to stay alive.

Her face was still pale. She kept seeing the tire iron. So did I.

"We're not," I said whispering. My hand went to my chest. The artifact was quiet now. Cold. Waiting. "We get the guns. We get the boat. We go."

"How?"

"The Man is neat, proud. He'll have our things in his room. A trophy."

It was a guess. A desperate one.

We waited until the deep night. Until the sounds of the guards on patrol were lazy, spaced apart. I had one weapon they missed. The knife I took from the thugs in the sunken park. I'd hidden it in my boot.

I slid it out. The metal was cool.

We moved like ghosts. Out of the room. Down a dark hall. The Man's door was unlocked. Arrogance.

Inside, it was neat. A cot. A desk. On the desk, our things. The glocks. The rifle. My knife. And our cans of food.

Sol grabbed the packs, started stuffing them. I went for the guns. My fingers closed around the grip of a glock.

A floorboard creaked behind us.

Boot-Face stood in the doorway. He wasn't smiling now. His shotgun was raised.

The room shrank around us. The air turned heavy, thick with the smell of oil and dust. My heart hammered in my ears. Sol froze, clutching the backpack against her chest like it could shield her. The artifact stirred inside me—not with fire but with a low, cold hum—as if it already knew what had to happen.

"He thought you might be stupid," he growled.

He didn't yell. He didn't need to. He just leveled the shotgun at Sol.

I moved. Not with thought. With instinct. I threw myself to the side, not at him, toward the wall.

The shotgun roared. The sound was monstrous in the small room. Plaster exploded next to Sol's head.

She dropped, scrambling behind the desk.

Boot-Face worked the pump. The spent shell clattered on the floor.

He turned toward the desk. Toward her.

He didn't see me coming from the side.

I didn't shoot. I didn't have time. I just slammed into him. We crashed into the doorframe. He was strong. He smelled of sweat and tobacco. He grunted, driving an elbow into my ribs. Pain exploded. My breath left me.

He tried to bring the shotgun around.

I brought my knife up.

I didn't stab. I sawed. Across his throat.

It wasn't clean. It wasn't deep. It was a ragged, tearing motion.
He made a sound. A wet, surprised gasp. A horrible gurgle. Hot blood
poured over my hand. Slick. Hot. He dropped the shotgun. His hands went to
his neck, trying to hold the red line together. His eyes were wide. Scared.

Just a man.

He sank to his knees. Then onto his side. He kicked twice, then was still.

The silence was louder than the gunshot.

Shouts echoed from outside. Running feet.

Sol stared at the body. At the blood pooling on the clean floor.

"Oscar," she breathed.

I grabbed the glock from the desk. "Go. Now."

We ran. Out the door. Into the night. A guard rounded the corner. I
didn't aim. I just pointed the glock and fired. The shot was deafening. The man
cried out, spun, fell into the water.

We ran for the dock.

Shots rang out behind us. Muzzle flashes in the dark.

We were almost there. The airboat was twenty feet away.

Sol was ahead of me. A figure rose up from behind a crate. A guard. He
raised his rifle.

I fired. Missed.

He fired.

The shot hit Sol in the back. She didn't cry out. She just made a sound. "Hunff." Like the air was punched from her lungs. She stumbled forward. Fell to her knees at the edge of the dock.

I shot the guard. He went down.

I ran to Sol. Her eyes were wide. Shock. She was trying to breathe. Blood bloomed on her shirt, dark and wet.

"Get up," I begged. "Sol, get up."

I grabbed her under the arms. Hauled her up. She was dead weight. Her legs wouldn't work.

More shouts. More shots. The water around us spat with bullets.

I dragged her toward the boat. Almost there.

A bullet sparked off the metal hull right next to us.

Sol flinched. Her foot slipped on the wet wood.

She fell. Not into the boat. Into the water.

Chapter 14: The Choice in the Water

She disappeared under the black surface.

I didn't think. I jumped.

The water was cold. A shock. I came up gasping. Sol surfaced next to me, choking. Her blood clouded the water around us. So much blood.

"I've got you," I grunted, looping an arm around her chest. "I've got you." I kicked toward the boat. It was only feet away. A million miles.

Sol's head lolled against my shoulder. Her breathing was a wet rasp.

Then I felt it. A movement in the water. Not from us. A pressure wave. A deep, silent displacement.

I froze.

They came from the deep gloom. Two of them. Bull alligators. Huge. Ancient. Their eyes were black beads above the water. They didn't swim. They glided. Drawn by the blood. By the thrashing.

Time slowed.

The larger one opened its mouth. Not a bite. A yawn. A cavern of teeth. Pale. Endless.

It moved fast. Unbelievably fast.

It didn't go for me. It went for the blood. For Sol.

Its jaws closed around her middle.

There was a sound. A crunch. A terrible, final sound of something vital giving way.

Sol's eyes met mine. For a fraction of a second. There was no fear. Just a final, profound surprise.

Then the gator rolled.

The world exploded into white water and red foam. I was thrown back. Smacked by the powerful tail. The water churned. I saw a flash of her arm. A strip of her shirt. A cloud of dark red expanding, consuming everything.

The other gator slid in. Tearing. Pulling.

I didn't see her anymore. I just saw them.

Their thrashing bodies. Their feast.

My mind broke. Pure animal terror took over.

I scrambled. Flailed. My hands hit the hull of the airboat. I clawed my way up. Fell into the bottom of the boat, gasping, vomiting water.

I looked back.

The water was settling. The red cloud slowly dissipated. A piece of cloth floated on the surface. Then it was pulled under.

They were gone. She was gone.

I fumbled for the ignition.

My hands were slick. With water. With her blood.

The engine roared to life.

I didn't look back. I shoved the throttle forward. The airboat leapt ahead. I fled into the dark. The sounds of the compound, the shots, the shouts—all faded behind me.

It was all replaced by the roar of the engine.

And then, by the sound of my own screaming.

Chapter 15: The Aftermath

I ran until the fuel light blinked red. I ran until the sun came up, gray and sickly.

I found a place to hide. The second story of a house. The roof was gone. The sky was my ceiling.

I got out of the boat. My legs gave way. I fell on the rotten carpet. I crawled to a corner.

I vomited until there was nothing left. Bile and saltwater.

I looked at my hands. They were stained brown with dried blood. Sol's blood. Boot-Face's blood.

I scrubbed them on my pants. It didn't come off.

I screamed.

A raw, ragged sound that tore from my throat. I screamed at the holes in the roof. I screamed at the gray sky. I screamed until my voice was gone.

Why? Why her? Why not me?

Where was the justice? Where was the fucking point?

I was a murderer. I cut a man's throat. I watched a woman get torn apart.

I ran.

I was damned. I knew it. I felt it in my soul. There was no God here. Only teeth. Only blood. Only the silent, indifferent water.

I pulled the artifact from my shirt. I held it in my filthy hands. I wanted to throw it into the water. I wanted to crush it.

"Why?" I croaked, my voice a wreck. "What is this for? What good is it? It didn't save her! It didn't save anyone!"

I expected heat. I expected a vision.

I got nothing. It was cold. Silent. Just a piece of carved rock.

I slumped against the wall. Empty. I had nothing left. No hope. No faith. No strength.

Then, a whisper. Not in my ears. In my mind. Amara's voice. Cool. Clear. A current in the silence.

You ask the wrong questions, Oscar Fuentes.

I flinched.

"What are the right questions?" I whispered to the empty room.

Do not ask for comfort. There is none. Do not ask for meaning. You must make it. You measure your soul by a world that drowned. Your morality is a ghost. It is a luxury you can no longer afford.

"She died because of me."

She died. You live. This is not a question of good or evil. It is a fact. You are the Keeper. The story does not end with your guilt. It continues with your breath.

I looked at the artifact. It began to pulse. A slow, steady rhythm. Not warm. Not cold. Just persistent. Alive.

Your children are out there. The world is teeth. You must be harder. You must be colder. You must be the rock the water breaks against. Survive, Keeper. So the story can be told.

The voice faded. The pulse remained.

I sat there for a long time. I looked at my bloody hands. I didn't see a sinner. I didn't see a hero.

I saw a tool.

I got up. I found a bottle of muddy water. I drank. I took the glock. I cleaned it. I checked the ammunition.

I walked to the broken window. The drowned world stretched out, endless, gray, and terrible.

The artifact pulsed against my chest. A heartbeat.

I had no God. I had no goodness left.

I had a purpose.

I started the engine. The roar was a promise.

I would survive. I would find them.

And I would never flinch again.

Biscayne Whispers

Prologue: The Wedding Verse

The air was thick with the syrupy sweetness of gardenias and champagne. Detective Gutierrez, a bull in a borrowed suit, stood trapped by a potted palm, wishing for a cigarette and the straightforward misery of a crime scene. The wedding was his wife's cousin's, and his attendance was non-negotiable.

"You have the look of a man who listens to whispers for a living," a voice said beside him.

Gutierrez turned. A lean man with salt-stung eyes and hair blown back by an imaginary wind leaned against the wall. A vintage typewriter rested on a small table beside him. A sign read: **The Biscayne Poet. Your Story, in Verse.**

"I'm off duty," Gutierrez grunted.

"The best time for poetry," the man said, his fingers poised over the keys. "Give me three words. Any words. The first from your head."

Gutierrez sighed, thinking of the city waiting outside the manicured garden, of his desk, the endless cycle of his work. "Homicide. Boulevard. Bay."

The Poet's hands flew across the keys. Clack-clack-clack-ding. Clack-clack. He tore the sheet free and pressed it into Gutierrez's hand with a knowing smile. "For when you need it," he said, before melting back into the crowd.

Gutierrez glanced down at the page.

The Boulevard of broken dreams

leads to a Homicide in the Bay
where the truth floats, or so it seems.

He crumpled it into his pocket, a party trick from a weirdo. He forgot about it. Until tonight.

Chapter One: The Flute on the Bay

Detective Gutierrez hated the water. It wasn't that he couldn't swim—he could—it was that Biscayne Bay had a way of swallowing things and not giving them back. Cars. Guns. Lovers. Truth.

Tonight, it had taken a body.

The call came in just after midnight. A fisherman reported something floating near the seawall. By the time Gutierrez arrived, the corpse had already been pulled out—male, late thirties, lungs full of saltwater, face empty. Another drowning, they said. Another accident. But Gutierrez had been on the job long enough to know accidents didn't play that restless, haunting flute music in the back of his skull, the same sound carrying across the water from a typewriter.

The Bay was glassy, the skyline trembling on its surface like a guilty alibi. Out of the dark, he spotted a man in a small boat. Not fishing. Not rowing. Just sitting with a typewriter on his lap, tapping words into the night air.

"We have to stop meeting like this," the man called out, a faint smile on his lips. "At least the last time we had champagne."

Gutierrez recognized him. The Biscayne Poet. He waved him in. The Poet walked lazily, cigarette between his lips.

"You see anything tonight?" the detective asked.

The Poet squinted, like the question itself was a riddle. "I saw the moon lean down and kiss the Bay. I saw a man's reflection break into pieces. I saw silence rise from the water like a widow."

He typed a few words, tore the sheet, and handed it to Gutierrez.

The detective glanced at the page. It read:

The Bay keeps secrets
in the lungs of dreamers.

Gutierrez sighed. "I'm asking about the drowning. A body."

The Poet smiled, thin and knowing.

For a moment, Gutierrez felt the night fold in on itself. The distant traffic, the radios crackling from squad cars, the restless Bay, all of it faded until it was just the two of them—Detective and Poet—standing at the edge of something too large to name. Gutierrez hated when the Poet did this, made the world feel like a riddle instead of a crime scene.

"Detective, everybody is drowning. Some just float sooner than others."

Gutierrez stuffed the paper into his pocket, though he knew it would get lost in his laundry like everything else.

He told himself the Poet's words were nonsense, just smoke and mirrors dressed up as wisdom, but they clung to him anyway. The kind of line that didn't fade, but wormed its way into the quiet hours of a man's shift, showing up when the city slept and the Bay whispered back.

"Thanks," he said flatly, turning away.

The Poet tapped his keys again, the sound carried across the water like a flute, restless, haunting.

Gutierrez lit a cigarette and stared back at the Bay. The body was gone, carted off by the medics. But the water still looked hungry.

And for the first time in years, Detective Gutierrez thought maybe the Poet was right.

Chapter Two: The Biscayne Clue

By the next night, the Bay had settled into a different kind of silence. The body was gone, filed away at the morgue, but the water still seemed to hold its shape, like the memory of a weight pressing down.

Detective Gutierrez lit his cigarette and stared across the dark water.

At the end of the dead-end street, near the seawall, the Poet sat with legs dangling toward the tide. Typewriter on his lap, a beer in a paper bag at his side, and a vanilla Black & Mild smoldering between his fingers. Gutierrez approached him.

"You see anything tonight?" he asked, his voice low.

The Poet didn't answer at first. Instead, he typed a single sheet, tore it off, and handed it gently to the detective.

Gutierrez unfolded it. The words read:

Salt and shadows, whispers in tide,
the body tells what the waters hide.
Look where the sun never shines,
mark of life beneath mortal lines.

"Look at the body again," the Poet said softly. "Behind his ear. Bottom of his wrists. See if the water left any secrets there."

Gutierrez frowned but nodded.

At the morgue, he crouched over the corpse again. Fingers traced pale skin. Behind the ear—nothing. Wrists—bare. No tattoos.

Nothing to suggest any clue.

Hours later, back at the seawall, Gutierrez found the Poet waiting with his typewriter. The detective lit another cigarette, the memory of the morgue still clinging to him.

"Why'd you make me do that?" Gutierrez asked, irritation and suspicion in his tone. "Why'd you ask me to look for these things?"

The Poet leaned back, smoke curling from the Black & Mild. His eyes reflected the Bay like twin moons.

"I lost her," he said quietly. "Ten years ago. Right here in this water. She went down for a swim and never came back up." He paused, voice raw. "I thought...maybe it could be him."

Gutierrez exhaled, the cigarette smoke mingling with the salty breeze. "You mean... you thought the dead man was her?"

"Not exactly," the Poet said, tapping the typewriter. "I just thought, in some strange way, the Bay might've returned something I'd been waiting for. Answers float differently, Detective. Sometimes, they need a poet to catch them."

The detective thought back to the corpse when it was found, still pale and silent under the streetlamps. The water was calm. The Bay had no answers, just reflections of memory, loss, and maybe, a hint of something yet to be found.

The Poet typed again, softly, removing the detective from his memory with the clack of his keys

The tides remember what we forget,
the silence keeps what we regret.

Gutierrez pocketed the new note. He didn't understand it. But he didn't need to. Some truths in Miami didn't speak, they floated.

Chapter Three: Verse and Veracity

The rain came down on South Beach not in drops, but in sheets, washing the neon of Ocean Drive into bleeding smears of color. Detective Gutierrez sat in his car, watching the doorman of the 1 Hotel dash to help a guest with an umbrella. He was miles outside his jurisdiction, driven by a single, nagging piece of paper.

The poem from the wedding.

The Boulevard of broken dreams
leads to a Homicide in the Bay
where the truth floats, or so it seems.

He'd found it that morning, crumpled in a jacket pocket destined for the dry cleaner. Seeing the words now, after the body in the water, felt like reading a threat, an omen.

The hotel lobby was a temple of curated calm—reclaimed wood, hanging greenery, the soft hum of well-heeled guests. And there, in a corner nook, sat The Biscayne Poet at a small wooden desk, a vintage typewriter before him. A sign propped beside him read: **Poet-in-Residence. Your Story, in Verse.**

A young couple laughed as he handed them a freshly typed poem.

Gutierrez waited, dripping rain on the polished concrete floor. When the couple left, he approached.

"Dr. Gutierrez," the Poet said, not looking up from his machine. "South Beach, rain, a detective's trench coat…very Philip Marlowe." He typed a quick line. Clack-clack-clack-clack-ding.

"We need to talk about the poem," Gutierrez said, his voice low.

"Which one? I write so many."

"The one from the wedding. The one you wrote with my words. Homicide. Boulevard. Bay."

The Poet finally looked up, his eyes unreadable.

"Ah, that one. Did you like it?"

"The man that washed up. In the Bay. It was like your poem said."

The Poet's face shifted into an expression of genuine surprise, followed by concern.

"Detective… It was a poem. A metaphor. The 'homicide in the Bay' is the death of the day, the drowning of the sun. It's about the melancholy of a Miami night." He gestured to the window at the pouring rain. "It's art. Not…forensics."

Gutierrez leaned in, placing his hands on the desk.

"How did you know?"

"I didn't know anything," the Poet said, his tone firm but still calm. "You gave me three words that scream 'Miami noir.' I assembled them. That's my job. It's a coincidence. A tragic one."

He was good. His denial was smooth, practiced. But Gutierrez saw the slightest tension in his jaw, a flicker in his eyes that said he was choosing his words as carefully as he chose them for his verses.

"The body had marks," Gutierrez pressed. "You told me to look."

"And did you find them?" the Poet asked, turning the question to him.

Gutierrez didn't answer. He just stared, trying to read the man like a difficult page of text. The only sound was the gentle clack as the Poet typed a single, solitary line. He tore it free but didn't hand it over.

"I think you should go, Detective. Your jurisdiction, and your answers, are waiting for you across the Bay."

Gutierrez straightened up. He'd gotten nothing. Or maybe he'd gotten everything he needed. The denial itself was a clue. He turned and walked back into the rain, leaving the Poet in his dry, leafy sanctuary. He knew, with a certainty that settled in his gut, that the man was lying.

The rain-slicked streets shimmered like broken glass under the streetlamps. Gutierrez lit a cigarette, watching the smoke curl against the night.

Lies have a weight to them, he thought, *heavier than truth, because they had to be carried. And the Poet carried his like an old suitcase, worn, but never discarded.*

Somewhere in those verses, in the spaces between metaphors, was the shape of something real. Gutierrez just had to decide if he was hunting a killer, or a man haunted by ghosts too heavy to name.

The poem was a clue, and the Poet was the one who had planted it. The only question was why.

Chapter Four: The Crematorium Clue

Gutierrez visited Marlon, the corner pimp who waited tables at Denny's by day. He was in a back booth, nursing a coffee spiked with something stronger.

"I might've seen something…someone," Marlon slurred, eyes darting toward the door as if expecting someone. "That Biscayne Poet. Boxers, bloody T-shirt, knife, hammer. Back door of the crematorium. Midnight."

Gutierrez shook his head internally. *I can't believe this. The Poet out there at midnight, blood on his shirt, a knife and a hammer in his hands? Marlon's drunk and scared. But the details are too specific, too bizarre to be entirely invented.*

Gutierrez leaned back in the booth, the plastic seat groaning under his weight. The rain from earlier still clung to his shoes, making the tile slick, treacherous.

He thought about the Poet's hands, steady, precise, tapping words into permanence. Could those same hands swing a hammer, drive a blade? The Detective had seen stranger things. Miami had a way of bending men, corrupting them, turning dreamers into executioners. The idea chilled him more than he wanted to admit.

"You're sure?"

"Man, I see what I see," Marlon said, defensive. "Dude was lurkin'. Looked like he'd seen a ghost. Or made one."

Gutierrez left him there, the words turning over in his mind. *Did I notice bruising? Swollen lips on the Poet? No. But I can't rule him out.*

Glancing at his watch, 3:05 PM, Gutierrez's mouth went dry. He craved Cuban coffee. Strong. Black. Bitter. Just like the city. He headed toward a ventanita, drank his cafecito in one scalding shot, and as the caffeine hit his veins, a realization cut through the haze: *It's Thursday.*

He knew where to find the Poet. On Thursdays, he hosted an open mic poetry program at the bookstore in Coconut Grove. It was the one appointment the man kept religiously.

He headed toward the station, thinking of the Bay, bodies, and typewriters scattered with cryptic poetry.

He brought the Poet in. The interrogation room was stark, a world away from the soft hotel lobby. The Poet sat quietly, calm, tracing the ceiling's water stains with his eyes as if they were constellations.

Halfway through the questioning, a patrol officer whispered in Gutierrez's ear.

"Detective…two more bodies just pulled from the Bay. And Marlon…he just walked into the precinct. He's confessing to the murders. All of them."

Gutierrez turned back to the interrogation room. The Poet hadn't moved. A faint, unreadable smile played on his lips. Gutierrez removed the handcuffs.

For a brief second, their eyes locked, Detective and Poet, predator and prey, or maybe just two men circling the same abyss from different shores. Gutierrez felt it then—the quiet certainty that he was letting something dangerous slip through his fingers. But he couldn't prove it, Not yet. Procedure demanded release, but instinct whispered chains.

"You can go. I'll take you back to the bookstore," he said, the words ash in his mouth.

The Biscayne Poet nodded and walked out, leaving the room alive with the echo of lies.

Back at the bookstore, the Poet continued his performance as if none of it had happened. The stairs, the fight, the detective, the precinct, they had all been shadows in the sunlight.

Outside, Miami simmered under the August sun. Gutierrez lit a cigarette, thinking of the Bay, bodies, the mysterious typewriter, and the cryptic poetry left behind. Two men, two life journeys, converging in a haze of jazz, crime, and verse, one walking free, one carrying the weight of a lie.

Chapter Five: The Ghost in the Ink

Back at the station after returning the Poet to his open mic night, Gutierrez was left in the thick Miami heat, pondering. The air didn't move. It sat on his skin, heavy and wet as a shroud.

Marlon's confession was too neat. A drunk's rambling story, polished into a perfect, desperate lie. Gutierrez had seen it before, the quick, convenient end to a case that begged to be messy. The Bay didn't give up its secrets so easily, and neither did men like Marlon.

His phone buzzed. The medical examiner.

The two new bodies from the Bay.

"Detective," the M.E.'s voice was crisp, clinical. "Preliminary on your new floaters. Male, late thirties. Both with significant pre-submersion trauma. Blunt force. And…something else."

Gutierrez lit a cigarette, the flame a tiny defiance against the oppressive daylight. "What else?"

"Tattoos. Recently removed. Lasered into oblivion, but the skin remembers. Under the UV, we can see the ghosts. An anchor behind one's ear. A series of numbers on the other's wrist. Like they didn't want to be identified, even in death."

The words from the Poet's first note echoed in Gutierrez's mind, a cold finger tracing down his spine. *Look where the sun never shines. Mark of life beneath mortal lines.*

He hadn't been looking for ghosts. He'd been looking for ink.

"Run the patterns through the database," Gutierrez said, his voice rough.

He hung up and drove toward the crematorium, the site of the fire, the place where Marlon's story began. The building was a squat, soft-stained thing, its air still tasting of ash and cooked bone. The back door was scarred, a fresh padlock hanging from the hasp. But it was the dumpster that caught his eye. Something white fluttered from under its lid.

It was a typewriter page, torn and smudged with grease.

The fire cleanses what the water claims:
two names whispered in the flames.
But ash to ash is not the end.
Just a truth we choose to send.
Ask the man who lights the pyre
what burns away with his desire.

Gutierrez's mouth went dry. It was the taste of a story folding in on itself, of a confession meant to hide a deeper sin. The Poet wasn't just catching answers that floated. He was tossing them into the current himself. And Gutierrez was finally learning how to read the tides.

Chapter Six: Where the Sun Never Shines

The rain had stopped, leaving the city steaming. Gutierrez found The Biscayne Poet where he knew he would: at the end of a dead-end street in Coconut Grove, his tuxedo-black 1974 Dodge Dart parked nearby like a silent familiar. It was a place known only to locals and loners, with a perfect, postcard view of the Miami skyline across the water. The man wasn't typing. He was just staring, as if waiting.

Gutierrez didn't speak at first. He placed the grease-stained note from the crematorium dumpster on the typewriter.

"No more verses," Gutierrez said, his voice flat with exhaustion. "Just the truth. You knew about the tattoos because you'd been watching him for a decade. You knew where to look because you knew how he marked them. The anchor. The numbers. You knew he'd try to burn the evidence because you know his business. The crematorium isn't just his cover; it's his disposal site. And the Bay...the Bay is where he puts the ones he can't burn."

The Poet didn't look at him. His eyes remained fixed on the water, on the distant lights of the city.

The skyline flickered in his gaze, as though each tower carried a secret of its own. Gutierrez wondered if the Poet saw a city of glass and steel, or if he only saw a graveyard—each reflection another body sunk beneath the surface.

Silence stretched between them, heavy as the tide, pulling both men toward truths neither fully wanted to speak.

"His name is Alvaro Ruiz. He owns the Peaceful Repose Crematorium. Ten years ago, my sister, Elena, was dating him. She thought he was a businessman. She found out what he really did. Disposing of rivals for the Norteños. She threatened to go to the police."

Gutierrez felt his chest tighten. Stories like this had crossed his desk too many times—women who trusted the wrong men, who thought love was a shelter and found only ruin.

Miami was littered with ghosts like Elena, nameless to the city but unforgettable to those left behind. He understood then that this wasn't just a case for the Poet. It was penance.

His voice was a dry rasp, stripped of all poetry. "He took her for a swim right here. Said it was an accident. I knew it wasn't. But I had no proof. Only the Bay knew."

"So you became a witness," Gutierrez said. "You sat out here every night. Watching him."

"I heard things," the Poet whispered. "Echoes on the breeze. I saw his boat go out late for 'joyrides.' I saw the kind of men who went with him—enforcers, debt collectors, the kind with tattoos they'd later regret. I saw the ghosts in his ink before they were ghosts. I knew his pattern. But what's the testimony of a poet against a pillar of the community?"

The question lingered, and Gutierrez realized it was the same one he asked himself each time the rich walked free while the poor bled out in alleys. The Poet's words weren't a riddle anymore. They were an indictment, not only of Ruiz but of the city itself. And in that moment, Gutierrez felt the line blur between detective and witness, law and verse.

"I needed a detective to see it. I needed you to find the proof I never could…The wedding. The poems. Marlon's confession." the Poet said, his hollowed eyes locked on Gutierrez's. "*You* orchestrated all of it. Marlon is in debt to Ruiz. Ruiz forced him to confess. I knew he would. I knew you'd see through it. I gave you the words. You found the truth."

Gutierrez looked out at the skyline. The Poet had used him, manipulated the entire investigation. But he had done it for a truth that deserved to be found.

"It's enough for a warrant," Gutierrez said quietly. "For Ruiz. For everything."

The Poet nodded slowly. "Is it enough? Does it bring her back?"

The words hung like a stone in the air, pulling Gutierrez down into a silence he couldn't escape. He thought of all the cases closed with paperwork and body bags, all the families told to move on because justice had been served. Justice was a ledger, cold and clean. But grief…that never balanced.

He wasn't asking Gutierrez; he was asking the Bay.

Gutierrez had no answer for that. He placed the original wedding poem on the typewriter.

For the first time since this began, Gutierrez saw the paper not as evidence, but as a relic, fragile, stained with rain and fingerprints, carrying the weight of everything unsaid. It was proof, yes, but also a confession, prayer, and curse. He realized then that the Bay hadn't just given back its dead, it had given him a story too heavy to carry alone.

"It's closure. That's all we get."

The Poet looked at the poem, then out at the water. He slowly fed the paper into the typewriter and typed a single, final line at the bottom:

And the Bay, at last, gives back its dead.

He handed it to Gutierrez. The detective nodded, put it in his pocket, and walked away. This one, he wouldn't lose in the laundry.

The Poet remained, a silhouette against the water, finally silent. The Bay had no more secrets for him, and the flute that plagued Gutierrez's skull with an eerie sound finally stopped.

Chimney Smoke, Gunpoint Lizards and Sexy Mamas

It was the Summer of 2003, I was living in a very old and ugly apartment building between Biscayne Boulevard and NE 2nd Avenue, off of 33rd street. I had a bitter, mentally unstable landlord that walked around with a concealed weapon. I had a part-time gig at History–Miami, the old Historical Museum of Southern Florida. I would give guided tours of the permanent galleries and write historical theatre scripts for their Summer Camp program.

Every afternoon of that summer I would arrive home from work, and I remember noticing really shady people coming in and out of my building. Pimps and prostitutes, the same ones one would see walking the sidewalks while driving on the Boulevard.

This one time I was sitting on my writing chair, trying to figure out an ending to three of my stories when suddenly, the phone rang. I answered it.

"Hello?"

"Oscar?"

"Maybe..."

"Hey, this is your landlord."

"What do you want?"

"What do I want? I want my rent, you punk!"

I hung up. Couldn't really stand people cursing on the phone. Especially annoying landlords like mine. This was the worst landlord I ever had. Two days late from the first of the month, and he was already calling the cops on me.

There was a knock on the door. I picked up a bad reading on it, but answered it anyway. Opened it. It was my neighbor, the stripper. She was 75 years old. She had a six-pack of beer, Heineken. I let her in. she always wore a mini skirt, and the skin on her legs was all loose and hanging down. Her teeth were yellow and twisted. She always bragged about how in her younger years, she was the hottest stripper in Miami, but now she was old, sick, and very tired. We drank the beer and talked about the poetry of life. I mentioned the BBQ smell in the building, and how it always smelled like BBQ.

She looked at me with frozen eyes, slowly pointed at my back window and said, "Oscar, there's a smoky chimney out there."

I got up to see and there it was, a smoky chimney right outside my window. I didn't ask her anything about it. I figured I would go down there and see for myself. After a while, she left. I kept on writing. The phone rang.

"Yeah?"

"Goddamn it, Oscar, I swear you hang up on me one more time, I'll put a bomb on your door knob" It was my landlord again.

"What do you want? You want my rent?"

"My rent! I want MY rent!!"

"Come pick it up."

"At what time?"

"Come now, you lizard."

"Oscar, if I go there and I don't find you, I swear to God I…"

I hung up on him again. Couldn't really stand people bitching on the phone. Someone knocked on my door. Someone knocked three times. I opened it.

It was a giant lizard wearing funky sunglasses, shorts, sandals, and a funny haircut. It also looked like an iguana, but it was my landlord.

"What are you doing here?"

"Oscar, I had it up to here with you." He pointed at his stomach.

He was a very tall man. Always smoking a cigar. Heavy set, about 300 pounds. With a heavy breath. Minty breath. Tobacco minty breath. He looked insane and dangerous.

"Your rent is five days late, Oscar!" He screamed, taking out his .45 caliber. He pointed the gun at my left knee. I froze. I didn't want to move. He walked around me, and now he was inside my apartment, pointing that thing at my back.

"I want my money, Oscar. Where is my money?"

"Look, Pops, just take it easy."

"I've been taking it easy for the longest."

"Look, man, I don't have your money here in the apartment."

"What?"

"Gotta take a drive to the bank on Coral Way, and my car's out of gas."

"That's no problem, we'll go in mine."

We left the apartment. He drove his car and steered the wheel with his left hand, while he pointed the .45 at my stomach with his right. I didn't even give him directions to the bank, and he knew all those short cuts to it. A speed driving lizard. One of those lizards you see on the road driving in rage, looking around, trying to find someone to hit with their bumpers. And he did. He hit an old lady crossing the street. She looked like my neighbor, the stripper. I looked. Wasn't her. I looked again. She was already up and walking, as if nothing.

We finally got to the bank. It was closed. Most banks closed around 5:00 in the afternoon; it was 4:45 pm. The lizard made me knock on the front glass door of the bank. The employees saw me knocking didn't even look twice. They all stood there counting their money. Thank God it was closed. My bank account was empty. Suddenly my chance to kick the gun off his hand came my way. His eyes opened wide, he couldn't believe I had just kicked that thing off his hand. I picked it up fast, and aimed it. I could smell the shit running down his pants.

"This is where you lose, lizard."

"You got a bomb on your door knob, Oscar."

"That's why you're going to open it for me."

"In your wildest dreams!" He screamed, as he ran away from me with surprising speed.

The coward. The yellow lizard. One of those sorry ass lizards you find in your back yard. I looked at my watch. It was already 5:15 on the dot. I remembered I had a date to attend with a hot mama. The hottest ever. I walked over to the lizard's car. He had left the keys in it. Got in. turned it on, and drove off into the congested streets.

Back at the apartment, I stood outside, and tried to come up with an idea. A solution. There was a 50% chance I had a bomb on my doorknob, so I broke in through the kitchen window. I noticed from inside the apartment that the doorknob had a black plastic device with a blinking light. It looked like a toy bomb. I walked up to it, and indeed. A toy bomb. I laughed, and I knew my landlord had lost his mind. It had an on/off button; I pushed it off and dropped it on the wooden floor. I laughed again. Took a quick shower. Got dressed, and heard the engine of my date's car pulling into the parking space. Without thinking there could have been a real bomb on the other side of the door, I walked towards it and opened it, walked out, closed it behind me, and locked it. And there I was, opening the door of the car and getting in. And there she was, switching radio stations and looking at me.

"Where to?" she asked.

"The Port. The City Port," I said.

"Why there?" she asked again.

"Sweetness, I really don't care where we go, anywhere you want is fine."

She smiled at me, and with her smile she showed me her beautiful teeth. She then stopped smiling and pointed at the building next to mine, asking: What is that smoky chimney I wonder?

We drove around the block on NE 2nd Ave to see what building was the one with the chimney. We looked and it read, Van Orsdel Crematorium. I sat in her car feeling shocked. It all made morbid sense. The dust on my window sill was no dust and the BBQ smell that circulated the hallways was no BBQ.

Iguanas, Leeches and Bloodlines

Imagine it's 1995 in Miami. The sun is setting, casting that beautiful, hazy orange glow over everything, the kind that makes the city look like it's on fire. I'm driving west down NW 36th Street, heading into the heart of Miami's neighborhoods, the streets a patchwork of sounds, smells, and people congregating at the *ventanitas* that serve Cuban coffee shots. As I turn south on Northwest 27th Avenue, I merge onto the bridge, and that's when I see him.

At first, it's hard to make sense of what I'm looking at. A man stands on the right side of the road, entirely covered in mud, clutching something massive in his arms. I slow down, as does everyone else, and through my passenger window, I get a good look. The man—mud dripping from his face, caked to his boxers, is holding a giant iguana in an embrace.

It's a wild, surreal sight, and I murmur to myself, "Oh, shit… That looks like my fucking uncle."

Yep, you heard right—my uncle. Untamed, raw, a force of nature in his own right. Growing up, I'd always thought I was different from him, like I didn't carry that same streak of wildness. But maybe, and perhaps, deep, deep…deep down, a part of that untamed spirit lived in me too.

I kept on driving, that image stuck in my mind. Later that day, he told me the whole story over a pack of Camel cigarettes.

It all started when he was crossing the Miami River with his buddy, Beto. They were cruising along, not a care in the world, when my uncle spotted it—an enormous and delicious iguana sunbathing on the top of a tree branch that hung over the water, a prize if there ever was one. Without a second thought, he yelled for Beto to pull over, and they quietly parked by a park. My uncle, always one to follow his instincts, walked nonchalantly around under the bridge, stripped off his boxers and waded into the mud-slicked river, determined to catch that iguana. What he hadn't counted on was how much of the "water" was actually thick, sticky mud.

When he was in position, he signaled to Beto, motioning for him to scare the iguana out of the tree. Beto did as told, and in a flash, the creature leapt from the branch with jaws wide, sharp white teeth flashing, diving straight at my uncle's head. My uncle caught it mid-air, but the iguana was so big and powerful that it pulled him under, sinking him deeper into the muck as they wrestled, man and beast locked in a muddy struggle.

The commotion must have looked insane to anyone nearby. Sure enough, a neighbor from a retirement home had seen the whole scene and called the cops. By the time my uncle stumbled out of the muck, victorious, the police were waiting for him.

He stood there, mud-caked, leeches clinging to his skin, and the officers, unsure how to react, finally asked what he planned to do with the iguana.

"I'm going to eat it," my uncle replied, dead serious.

The officers exchanged glances. One of them commented that he'd heard iguana meat was a delicacy in some parts, but they urged my uncle to let the creature go, explaining that the locals had a certain fondness for the iguanas. Reluctantly, he released it, watching as it slipped back into the water, like a small, scaly alligator.

"Thank you, sir, you can go home now," one of the officers said.

The officers, still standing by the bridge, watch my uncle as he begins to move away, but their attention is drawn to something that wasn't there before. A subtle glint of red. It's small at first, a trickle, but enough for them to notice.

"Sir, there's blood on your body," one of the officers says, his tone more urgent now. "There's a little bit of blood coming out of you. What's going on?"

Before my uncle can even respond, his friend Beto, who has been standing off to the side watching the scene unfold, suddenly points at my uncle's back. "Hey, Salvador! You have leeches on your body!"

Leeches? My uncle freezes mid-step, his brow furrowing as the realization hits him. He looks down at his arms, at his legs, at his back—and that's when he sees them. These enormous, thick leeches, clinging to his body like silent, insidious parasites. They're long—three to four inches at least—and their bodies are bloated, swollen with the blood they've been sucking out of him. They're everywhere. His arms, his sides, his legs.

The officers step back a bit, their faces twisting in both shock and discomfort. "You've got to get those off," one of them says, his voice now full of concern. "You're going to get sick from that. You need to wash yourself immediately before you get an infection."

But my uncle doesn't seem phased. He just shrugs, his usual nonchalance creeping back into his demeanor. "Ah, don't worry about it," he says, brushing it off like it's no big deal. "This is nothing."

He reaches down and starts rubbing his hands over the leeches, slowly but steadily pulling them off one by one, squeezing them between his fingers and throwing them to the side. The mud and blood mix together, creating a grotesque smear on his hands. He walks over to a nearby coconut tree, and with a smooth motion, begins to rub his back against the bark, trying to scrape the remaining leeches off.

The sight is unreal. The blood and mud smear against the rough tree, dripping down onto the ground in streaks. The officers, standing nearby, can only watch in stunned silence as my uncle goes about his business as if he's done this a hundred times before. His back is raw against the tree as he scrubs the last of the leeches off, and when he straightens up, there's blood dripping from the raw areas on his skin where the leeches had been.

The smell of mud, blood, and sweat hangs heavy in the air, and for a moment, the scene feels surreal. It's one of those strange, uncomfortable moments in life that doesn't quite fit into reality. There's something primal about it, something that feels like it belongs in another world.

Finally, my uncle stands up, wiping his hands on his pants, looking at the officers. "See? No big deal," he says, with a grin that's almost too casual for someone who just had leeches feeding on him in a muddy river. The officers exchange a glance, unsure of how to respond to the bizarre turn of events.

"Alright, sir," the officer says slowly, still processing what he's just witnessed. "Just… be careful. Go wash up. That could've been dangerous."

My uncle just nods, a flicker of amusement in his eyes. "I'll be fine," he mutters, turning away. He starts walking back toward his car, the mud still drying on his body, and Beto follows behind him, shaking his head in disbelief.

For the officers, it's just another bizarre day in Miami, but for my uncle, it's just another story to add to the collection. A man, a giant iguana, some leeches, and a whole lot of mud—just another thing he lived and experienced.

See, it's that wild energy, that instinct to survive on his own terms, was woven into the fabric of who he was.

These days, each time I drive down 27th Avenue and over that bridge, I can't help but wonder—how much of him is in me? Am I as untamed as my uncle Salvador? Is that same Crocodile Dundee spirit hidden somewhere in me, waiting for the right moment or iguana to surface? I don't know yet. I don't know. To me, my uncle Salvador is the living difference between boys and men. I don't care what anybody says.

The Cock Fight

I once attended a cock fight in Honduras. Many men waited for the cock-fighting circus to arrive. Eager owners gave rigorous training to their best roosters all year. People respected those owners, who were known for their prime fighting cocks.

On the small, seasoned patio where the event was held, one corner awaited the arrival of the cocks' cages. Inside, roosters insulted each other with their songs. While the fighting roosters screamed their cock-a-doodle songs, people moved onto the patio, the home of the humble man who offered to build the fight ring and host the event.

The ring was built in the center of his patio. Surrounding it were wooden stools and chairs he made. The ring consisted of long strips of plywood around a circular frame. The floor was covered with sawdust, chips of cedar, and a dusting of pine.

In the corner opposite the roosters sat the humble man's wife, a passive woman, similar to many who lived in the village. She stood behind a wooden counter selling oranges, tropical fruit, and beer. The fanatic cock fighters drank so much beer, it seemed the event would never start.

When the beer was finally consumed and the cock fighters were all drunk, they lay on the floor. I imagined they were dead, because they lay without a word. Even the roosters were asleep. The only ones awake were the humble owner's wife and me.

She seemed angry, as if she were thinking, *The motherfucker! The fucking guy offers to host the event, builds a ring, gets drunk with his cock-fighting friends, and then forgets the whole thing!*

Grabbing an empty beer bottle, she slammed it against the six-foot concrete wall behind her. At the sound of the bottle exploding, the men woke up like killer bees snapping out of their daily work in the hive when someone hit it with a rock.

Immediately, her husband got into the center of the ring and said, *"Beinvenidos sean todos los galleros que se encuentran aqui presente. Mucha suerte, y que empieze la pelea de gallos! Hijos de puta!"*

The cock fighters cheered loudly, and two jumped into the ring carrying roosters. They shook hands and let the roosters see each other. The birds, instantly ready to fight, were beautiful, more elegant than eagles.

The men in the ring signaled each other and tossed their birds into the air, as the audience cheered. In the corner where the cages waited, the roosters seemed to meditate on the crowd's noise, but they were totally quiet.

For a moment, time seemed to freeze. We all sat motionless, our mouths open, staring at the birds in the air. They seemed to float three or four feet above the center of the ring, stabbing at each other. When they connected and disconnected, sharp spurs pierced each other's bodies.

For a few moments, they battled in the air, then one landed on the floor head first, almost dead, spitting blood. Scarlet red stained the yellow sawdust covering the floor.

The victor glided down to the floor with elegance and grace, creating gusts of wind by flapping his wings and sending sawdust everywhere in a cloud that blocked all visibility. The crowd totally silent, as the victor folded his wings and sang his victory song. The cocks in the cages added their voices to the chaos.

The audience returned to normal. The host's wife received another keg of beer, and the men formed a line in front of the counter. I found a homemade stool and sat on it, knowing it would be a while before the next match began.

Payaso

The clown did not hesitate.

He ran out of the circus really fast, looked up into the sky, and it was blue, the same as the day before. Different clouds, but still the same blue. He had a permanent smile that could charm any living creature on earth. He walked and looked around for a while, and there she was, coming out of her yellow door, and the door closing behind her, also wearing a permanent smile.

She had a smile that tamed any furious beast on any circus grounds. They smiled at each other, walked toward each other, hugged, kissed, smiled again, held hands, and walked away from the performing area, heading towards the woods. Now they were in and under the trees, with rays of light beaming through the leaves.

For about twenty minutes, they walked until they reached the edge of the lake. She sat on a wooden bench facing the water, and he stood behind her, rubbing her shoulders. Facing the lake and smiling at it, they both remained silent for a moment, but just for a moment.

"What are you thinking, Oscar?"

"I'm thinking about the unfortunate treatment animals get at the circus."

"Don't break your head over that, baby; there's nothing we can do."

"It really bothers me, Olga."

"It bothers me too."

"But not as much as it bothers me."

"You don't know that."

"Yes, I do."

"No, you don't."

"Yes, I do. I notice it every time you do your act."

"Oh yeah?"

"Yeah."

"Get out of town."

"I'm serious. You know that part in your act when you're making the lion walk on his back legs?"

"Yes?"

"And how you make him walk and run around the ring, till his tongue hangs all the way down?"

"Yeah, and?"

"You mistreat the animal too, Olga."

"The lion likes it."

"He doesn't like it."

"He hasn't bitten me."

"Yet."

"That giant cat is in love with me."

"The fool. Poor thing, you're making him believe he's going to get a piece of ass. Poor thing. He'll eat you when he finds out you've been messing with his head."

She stood up from the bench and started toward the circus without saying a word. Oscar followed her at a slower pace. Olga walked out of the woods and headed toward the lion's cage.

The lion, inside his cage, slept like a baby. He gave silent roars for snores. He was fifteen feet long, nine hundred fifty pounds, with a hairy black spot on the tip of his tail and a ten-year-old beard that stretched all the way up his head and around his ears. This beard hung long and low, all the way down to the floor. But now he was asleep, resting carelessly inside his cage, releasing silent roars for snores. You could hear the beast breathing in and out.

Olga walked up to the cage. The cat opened his mind-reading eyes, stared at Olga, who had an enchanting beauty, probably the most beautiful woman on earth.

"Hello there, my beautiful lion," Olga said to the fifteen-foot-long cat. "Why do you always have a serious look on your face, huh?"

She continued, "No, don't get up; do you mind if I come in and lie by your side?"

The animal sat on his two back legs and lowered his chest, lowering his majestic head. She opened the gate slowly, got in, closed the gate behind her, got on her knees, and rested her body against the lion. Twenty minutes went by. Twenty-five minutes went by. And out from the woods came Oscar the clown.

With a permanent smile, he walked toward the lion's cage. He noticed Olga sleeping with the lion. The giant cat stood up fast on his four legs. Olga's body flew against the thin bars of the cage.

"What the hell's wrong with you?" Olga screamed at the beast.

The animal grinned at Oscar, showed Oscar his long sharp teeth. Oscar noticed the lion smiling. He kept on walking towards the cage. The lion sneezed, then gave a roar—an earthquake of a roar. Everything shook when the beast awakened. Oscar's heartbeat raced. His feet did not move him forward or backward. He just stood there somewhere between the woods and the cage. His knees shook like earthquake waves. Cold sweat ran down his forehead.

Olga stared at Oscar, stared and stared and stared, and laughed. Olga laughed a sinister laugh. She didn't really care for Oscar's feelings. Oscar the clown noticed the angry lion. The animal released clouds of steam from his ears. The cat gave another roar. Oscar's legs did not move; they seemed to be frozen in the most awkward position. Cold sweat was now running down his entire body, and he had about twenty knots in his throat. Oscar tried swallowing but was not able. The lion was angrier than ever, the angriest. He didn't like Oscar, felt insecure around him, especially when Olga was around. The cat was very well aware that he was just an animal, unable to transmit human emotion. Oscar had the upper hand, and Oscar the clown knew this, for he had made love to Olga many times before, but now she was inside the cage, and the woman inside the cage was Oscar's lady.

Not a moment more went by when the lion gave another aggressive roar. This roar was louder than the two he had given before. Everyone inside the circus tents rushed out towards the lion's cage. Oscar was still standing somewhere between the woods and the cage.

All the circus freaks surrounded Oscar the clown, and I mean, all the freaks: the earless midget, the twelve-foot-thin man, the flying acrobats with wings, the six-legged man, the 6-year-old Cuban boy with a communist father, the ugliest man on the planet Fidel Castro, the manatee man, the talking rabbit, the four hundred fifty-pound man, the magician, the wolf man, the President of the United States, OJ Simpson, the Colombian mafia, and standing right next to Oscar the Clown, Medusa, with thirty poisonous snakes for hair.

Everyone just stood there, next to and behind Oscar, staring at the most beautiful woman on Earth and at the most beautiful lion. Everyone mumbled their judgmental slurs. Then Olga whispered something in the cat's ear. All the freaks got quiet. You could even hear the wind whistle in the ear. The fifteen individuals that surrounded Oscar took one step backward. Oscar remained still. His legs still frozen. Everyone noticed how Olga slowly unlocked the lion's cage, opened it, and oh, how she left it wide open. All the freaks took five steps back. Except Oscar. Olga jumped out of the cage. The lion jumped out of the cage. Olga whispered one last thing into the lion's ear.

"Olga, get him inside the cage right now!" Oscar announced.

"Tell your monster friends to step back under the tents, huh?"

"Alright, you all heard her!" Oscar told his mob of freaks.

They all went back under the circus tents, back to their business. Olga started towards Oscar, and the lion followed her closely. Oscar did the same, and the two of them were now just six feet away from each other. The freaks inside the colorful tents pretended to mind their own business, but they didn't. They were all twisting their eyes toward the outside and kept their ears sharp on the event that went along out in the open.

Olga and the lion stood side by side, and Oscar stood in front of them. The lion sat on his hind legs as if waiting for Olga to let him know that it was okay to eat him. The fifteen-foot-long cat was hungry. Oscar could hear the hunger roars the lion's stomach made.

Olga grabbed the lion's cheeks and gave the cat a kiss on his hairy mouth. She gave him tongue. Oscar noticed. The lion opened his eyes wider and wider. Olga kept on kissing and kissing. Oscar the clown was now very jealous, furious, insulted, turning red in the face. Forehead sweating bullets. Sweating from the palms of his hands. Unable to interrupt the kiss because an interruption in this case would mean death. Painful death. Oscar felt helpless. The lion had the upper hand now. Or maybe the cat always did have the upper hand, who knows? Who knew? The gorgeous Olga was the only one who knew the upper hand man. Oscar was confused.

The lion was now breathing heavily, and his heartbeat was unstoppable. Fast. Faster. Breathing heavier. Olga kept kissing and kissing.

"You're going to give him a heart attack, Olga. STOP KISSING HIM!" Oscar screamed.

The lion's eyes were now closed. His two front legs were shaking. The giant cat had lost most of his mighty strength. Olga stopped kissing him. She took one step back. Moments passed, and the animal's body tumbled onto the grassy ground.

"You killed him!"

"He's not dead, he's asleep."

"What were you thinking, Olga?"

"I was going to feed him a beautiful clown."

"I'm leaving the circus."

"What?"

"I don't want to be a part of it anymore."

"Oh, did I scare you?"

"You're not funny, Olga."

"I'm not?"

"And you're not as beautiful as I thought."

"It was only a stupid joke, Oscar."

"Then I don't understand your sense of humor; I'm leaving."

Oscar took one step back, turned around, and started walking towards his little trailer. Olga's trailer was right next to his. Oscar's trailer was the one with the blue door.

A Forgotten Friend

Oscar Senior took a ride on his bike. Gloria had decided to take the bus because she felt too old to ride on the bike with Oscar.

The humble light-blue house of Josefina, Gloria's mother, was six miles away from their home. They both had gone to visit the old folks—it had been a while since they last saw each other. Actually, Josefina had been sick for quite a long while. She had gotten the flu really bad, her knees had gone weak, and the veins on her legs had thickened—blue, sometimes purple—but her daughter had come over with Oscar, and she was going to be okay.

Gloria had gone to nursing school, and she really knew how to handle the injection needle. Who knows exactly how many injections she had given to people; everyone in their neighborhood knew she was a certified nurse, and most of them had gone to her house once or twice for an injection or two.

Now, Gloria found herself inside her mother's house, the same exact house she had lived in ever since she was a little girl. After fifty-some years, she was back in the old house, and as she injected the antibiotic into her mother's left arm, Gloria thought about her childhood. She thought about the many little details engraved in her memory—the walls of her mother's house, the old tile floor, the high ceilings, her long-lost friends, her five sisters, and her two brothers. She thought about them as little girls and boys, and she thought about time—how it had gone by so fast. Gloria thought about her three kids, and how each of them had started their own family life. She thought about Oscar Junior and his pregnant girlfriend, and the baby boy inside her belly.

"What are you thinking about, mama?" Josefina asked.

"My son. I'm thinking about my son."

"Which one, Carlos?"

"No. Oscar. Wow, I can't believe he's having a baby boy."

"Yeah, me neither."

Gloria had already injected the antibiotic into her mother's arm, and an hour had just passed since she'd arrived at the old house.

"Look, there comes your husband."

"Where?"

"There." Josefina pointed with her right arm toward the outside. Her left arm felt numb, with a constant electric shock of pain.

Gloria looked through the windows and kept her eyes on Oscar.

Oscar rode his bike down a little hill where the main street pavement had been laid, about fifty feet in front of Josefina's old house.

He maneuvered his bicycle and stopped it right at the front gate. Got off. Parked it under the tropical shade of an almond tree. Opened the front gate slowly and walked in under the tin roof of the front porch.

Oscar walked into the house through the front door, feeling out of breath. His legs felt weak, and sweat slowly ran down both sides of his forehead.

"You had me worried there for a moment, my love," Gloria said to him.

"I'm okay, my princess. It's been a while since I last rode that bicycle."

"I know," Gloria replied.

"Why don't you sit down and rest? I'll make you a coffee," said Josefina.

"Thank you," Oscar replied.

He sat down on Josefina's old, comfortable couch and took a deep breath. Then he sighed.

Josefina, with caution, stepped down into the kitchen, which was at a lower level than the living room, and started heating the water for coffee. Gloria and Oscar sat by themselves under the living room ceiling and looked at each other. Gloria smiled at him. He smiled at her. They both had puppy eyes, and it was obvious that love was now stronger than ever.

After a while, Josefina walked back into the living room and handed Oscar a warm cup of good Honduran coffee. She sat next to him on the couch. Gloria sat at one of the chairs at the dining table. The three of them talked and laughed for a good while. And after five whole hours, they all felt tired. Oscar and Gloria decided it was time to head back to their small house.

They both kissed and hugged Josefina. Gloria gave her an extra hug, and they embraced tightly for a moment.

Meanwhile, Oscar stood outside the house, under the cool tropical shade of Josefina's almond tree, and thought about his cockfighting chickens. He thought about training them some more. Thought about taking them to competition. All his life, Oscar had been a fanatic of the cockfight. He owned seventy-two fighting roosters and sixty-three fighting hens.

Finally, Gloria came out of her mother's house and closed the front gate behind her.

"Are you taking the bus again?" Oscar asked.

"Do you want me to go with you?" she asked.

"Only if you want, but it's a long ride. Maybe you should take the bus."

"Okay, I'll take the bus."

"I'll walk you to the bus stop."

They started walking toward the main street hill, and halfway there they both turned around and looked at the house, as if looking for Josefina. And she was there—standing behind the front gate of her house and under the tin roof of her porch. Gloria and Oscar waved. Josefina waved back. They kept on walking and started climbing the hill. Reached the main street. Crossed it, making sure there were no cars coming either way. They got to the bus stop. Oscar parked the bicycle off to the side. He held Gloria's hand. Gloria held his. They kissed. Smiled. And waited for the bus to come.

After a moment, the bus finally arrived. Gloria got in, paid her fare. The bus started moving. She looked out through the window, searching for her husband. He was still there. Standing. Waiting for her to look. He knew she would. And she had. They stared at each other and smiled. Oscar waved. Gloria didn't. And her bus was now very far away, heading toward their neighborhood.

Oscar unlocked the parking pedal of the bicycle. Walked it a bit. Then hopped on. Started pedaling. He was in motion. Slowly gaining speed. Now going fast—fast enough to feel and hear the wind in his ears.

Between Josefina's house and the house Gloria and Oscar owned, there were six miles of sugarcane plantation. While riding, Oscar settled into a comfortable pedaling rhythm without even noticing. There was a nice fresh afternoon feel to the air, and Oscar had not started to sweat. He had rested his knees for five hours, and they didn't feel weak—they felt strong. His knees felt young and light.

He rode on the narrow side of the main street that was dusty and kept the road to himself there, careful not to ride in the center lane—this part of town had a reputation for bad drivers. Oscar Senior had always preferred his horse ride over the bus ride because he knew too many people—or should I say, too many people knew him—and to avoid the small talk, he'd take the long way, because the long way was lonely and quiet and peaceful.

Halfway home, in the middle of all that sugarcane, Oscar stopped pedaling. Slowly, his bicycle coasted to a stop. It had been a long day and full of nothing. No action. The sun looked good—giant and orange. He felt a little out of breath, but that was okay.

Right where Oscar stopped, there in the middle of the road and the sugarcane, he gave a deep sigh and thought about his kids. Gloria's kids were the same kids Oscar thought of whenever he thought of his kids. Now he thought of the youngest—Carlos Antonio Fuentes—who had recently moved out and into a small, simple place he and his girlfriend had found on the skirt of Merendon Mountain.

"Goddamn it, Oscar, you did it," he said to himself.

The orange Central American sun was going down slow and majestic, and Oscar loved to catch the sun on its way down. Every day around this time, he made sure to be out in the open, looking toward it. But he would never look straight at the sun. Instead, he liked to contemplate the mix of colors in the Central American sky.

Today the sky looks nicer than yesterday, Oscar thought.

And while thinking that, he noticed how it was getting dark and late. So he pushed his bicycle forward, hopped on, and kept heading toward his house. The colors in the sky were fading. The sky was now not so pretty. And Oscar knew this, but still, he kept looking up while riding the old horse.

Then he heard a voice. The voice came from behind.

Oscar turned his head and looked back.

Someone was riding a bicycle toward him—but they were too far away to make out.

"Oscar!" the voice called again.

Oscar stopped completely. Turned. Waited.

The man got closer.

He looked familiar.

Oscar squinted, trying to recognize him.

Then the man spoke again—

Oscar turned. The sun hit his eyes.

He squinted. The man on the bike called his name again.

"Oscar!"

Oscar couldn't see his face. The light was too strong.

The man got closer.

It was Bonerges.

His childhood friend.

Oscar hadn't seen him in years.

They once rode a small boat together to the center of Ticamaya Lagoon. They scattered Bonerges' father's ashes that day. It was his father's birthday. A lightning storm broke open the sky. They never forgot it.

That same lagoon had almost drowned them once.

They were teenagers then. They had skipped school. The day was too beautiful to stay inside. A group of girls was going to the lagoon. They followed. Showed off. Ran into the water laughing, chasing each other.

They wore jeans.

Bad idea.

The jeans pulled them down fast. Like stones. They couldn't swim right. They panicked. Yelled. Water in their mouths.

One of the girls jumped in.

Lorena Duranza.

She swam hard and fast. She went under. Came up. Shouted, "Take off your pants! You're sinking!"

They did. Handed them to her.

She held their jeans in one hand and told them to swim.

They swam.

The other girls waited on the shore.

Laughing. Nervous. Clapping for Lorena.

Two skinny boys. Cold. Ashamed. Chicken skin on their arms. Hands covering themselves. Laughing. Embarrassed.

Now they walked together again. Pushing their bikes.

Quiet.

Remembering.

Oscar thought about Lorena.

He didn't say it out loud.

He just walked.

Poems

The Flame and the Flood

One city ends in water,
another in fire.
We are born of both elements,
the slow, cold, drowning regret
and the sudden, hot, consuming rage.
Our lives are a constant navigation
between these two extremes.
The flood that erases
and the fire that purges.
To be alive
is to be perpetually caught
between drowning and burning,
to feel the water rise
while smelling the smoke on the wind.
Our resilience is measured
not by escaping either,
but by learning to tread the churning surface
where the ash meets the foam.

The Artifact's Truth

Some truths are not meant to be held with bare hands.
They are white hot,
searing,
and elemental.
They demand a glove,
a barrier,
a ritual to be approached.
They do not offer comfort,
they offer purpose.
They torture you with visions of what you've lost,
only to provide a single, grim coordinate,
a grave that is also a starting line.
This truth is not a solace,
but a compass.
Its pulse a steady, insistent drumbeat against your chest,
pulling you through the murk.
It is a terrible gift,
but in a world of endless water,
a purpose, however painful,
is the only raft.

The Smoky Chimney

We build our lives in apartments
next door to the crematorium.
We notice a strange, sweet, BBQ smell in the hallways
and dismiss it.
We wipe a peculiar grey dust from our windowsills
and think nothing of it.
We choose the fiction
because the truth is too morbid to bear.
We ignore the smoky chimney
right outside our window
because to acknowledge it
is to acknowledge the constant, grinding machinery of endings
that operates just next door.
The central truth of existence
is not that we will die,
but that we are willing to live our entire lives
pretending the smoke
is just from a neighbor's grill.

The Door Knob's Blinking Light

We spend our lives
fearing the bomb on the other side of the door.
The consequence,
the confrontation,
the catastrophic end we are sure awaits us.
We tiptoe through our own hallways,
paralyzed by the imagined threat.
But when we finally dare to look,
to confront the source of our dread,
we often find it is just a toy.
A cheap plastic imitation of power,
operated by a pathetic and broken mind.
Our greatest terror
is frequently a hollow bluff.
Our liberation is not a grand battle,
but the simple, quiet act
of reaching out
and turning off the blinking light.

The Leech and the Iguana

There is a wildness in our blood,
an untamed, primal instinct
that sleeps deep within the civilized self.
It is the part that sees a giant iguana sunning itself
and thinks only,
"I will catch it.
I will eat it."
It is the part that wades
into the thick, sucking mud of life
without a second thought,
ready to wrestle something magnificent and dangerous.
We emerge caked in the muck of the struggle,
pulling the leeches of consequence from our skin,
the regrets,
the wounds,
the parasites of memory.
And we are proud,
not in spite of the scars,
but because of them.
They are the proof that we fought for something real,
something that made us feel alive.

The Luxury of Morality

In the drowned world,
the old maps are useless.
The rules we once lived by are relics,
sinking beneath the floodwaters.
Morality, in such a place,
is a ghost,
a luxury for those who still have a roof,
a full belly,
and the illusion of safety.
True survival demands a colder, harder calculus.
It is no longer a question of good or evil,
but of action and consequence.
It is the cut of a knife across a man's throat
to save a woman who will be taken anyway.
It is understanding that to be a sinner or a hero
is a binary for a world that no longer exists.
You are simply a tool,
and your only function is to endure.

The Cockfight's Elegance

We ritualize our violence.
We build rings of plywood
and sprinkle scented sawdust to absorb the blood,
dressing our brutality in ceremony.
We convince ourselves
there is art in the struggle,
grace in the kill,
honor in the gamble.
It is a necessary lie we tell
to make the raw, tearing reality of existence beautiful,
to give a semblance of meaning and order
to the spilled scarlet on the yellow floor.
The crowd's cheers are an incantation
against the randomness of death,
a fleeting belief
that this ending, at least,
has rules.

The Circus of Self

We are all performers
in the ragged circus of our own psyche,
surrounded by the freaks and monsters
of our deepest fears
and most desperate desires.
The lion of our rage paces in its cage,
majestic and terrifying,
only held in check
by the flimsy bars of our routine.
But then the one we love,
the tamer we trust,
whispers a secret into its ear
and slides the bolt open.
The performance is over.
The raw, hungry id leaps out,
and we are left frozen center stage,
a clown in makeup,
realizing the beautiful tamer
was never on our side to begin with.

The Unwritten Verse

We are all poets
at the mad typewriter of our own existence,
typing verses on a machine
we can never fully control.
The plot is chaos,
the characters drift in and out of the narrative without warning,
and the setting is a city
that is either burning or flooding.
We clutch at scraps of meaning,
at three words given to us by chance.
Homicide.
Boulevard.
Bay.
And try to assemble them into a coherent whole.
The ending is always a blank page,
waiting for the final, decisive clack of the keys.
And we can only hope
that when we tear the sheet free,
the poem doesn't read like an obituary.

The Typewriter's Ghost

We are haunted
by the ghosts of stories never finished,
letters never sent,
and truths never typed.
The keys of our memory clack
with the weight of every possibility,
every path not taken,
every word left unsaid.
These phantom narratives echo
in the trunk of our consciousness
like the restless spirits of dead writers,
their middle fingers eternally stuck in a curse
against the silence.
We carry these ghosts,
these unwritten verses,
and they shape our every step,
a constant, whispering reminder
of the lives we could have led.

The Forgotten Friend

Time is a long, lonely road
under a fading sky.
We pedal forward,
lost in the rhythm of our own thoughts,
the weight of our years
making our knees feel weak.
And then, a voice calls from behind,
a familiar echo cycling out of the past.
A forgotten friend,
a shared memory of nearly drowning in a lagoon,
of a lightning storm
and a father's ashes.
When they catch up,
you don't need to speak.
You just walk together,
pushing your bikes,
the shared silence
a more profound poem
than any that could be typed.
It is a fleeting reminder
that we are not alone on this road.
Our ghosts sometimes keep pace with us.

The Keeper's Burden

We are not the authors of our fate,
but its reluctant keepers.
The artifacts we are given,
guilt, love, memory, a literal carved stone,
have a pulse and a will of their own.
They choose us,
not the other way around.
Our struggle is not to command them,
but to listen.
To heed their rhythm in the dark,
to feel their warmth against our chest
when all else is cold.
The burden is not the weight of the thing itself,
but the terrifying responsibility of its voice.
Our only choice is to carry it,
to let its story continue through our breath,
or to be drowned by its silence.

On the Bay's Indifference

The Bay is the ultimate existential witness.
It does not judge,
mourn,
or remember.
It simply is.
It holds lovers and corpses,
poets and thieves,
with the same silent, immense embrace.
It accepts our offerings:
our secrets,
our sins,
our discarded evidence.
Our screams for justice,
for meaning,
for revenge,
are merely ripples on its surface.
A surface that much prefers
to perfectly reflect the moody, beautiful,
and uncaring sky.
To ask it for answers
is to misunderstand its nature.
The Bay does not give,
it only receives.

The Airboat's Solitude

In the endless water,
you are your own island.
The roar of the engine is not just propulsion,
it is a declaration of self
against the vast, silent, consuming world.
It is the sound of your own will,
a mechanical prayer screamed into the void.
In this new lawless sea,
where every man is a thief
and every shadow a threat,
the greatest thing you can steal
is not supplies or fuel,
but another day of solitary autonomy,
another moment of pure, uncompromised
forward motion into the unknown.

The Measure of Ghosts

We spend our lives taking measurements in a sunken house,
tracing the height marks on a doorframe
that now exists only in memory.
We search for proof of a life we didn't live,
milestones we missed,
faces that have become strangers in a photograph.
But the past is a flooded neighborhood,
a lost paradise we can only visit
by holding our breath
and diving into the murky, painful depths.
We are all measuring ghosts,
trying to quantify a love or a loss
that the indifferent water has already claimed.
We surface gasping,
clutching not an answer,
but the cold, slippery fact of its absence.

Acknowledgements

I am thankful to the Miami literary community that has embraced my creative work through the decades, and to the lasting friendships and partnerships that have, in so many ways, nurtured and supported my creative career. Success is never a singular thing, it is a collective effort. And I am deeply grateful to everyone who has encouraged me to keep doing what I love.

I am especially grateful to my family for their unwavering support throughout this journey. Your encouragement and love have always been my foundation. I also want to extend a heartfelt thank you to J.J. and David from Jitney Books for believing in me and inviting me along on this journey with *Biscayne Inferno*.

The stories within this collection are a love letter to the magical city of Miami. Every corner of this vibrant place has served as a source of creative inspiration.

Thank you all for being part of this adventure.

ABOUT THE AUTHOR

Oscar Fuentes, known as The Biscayne Poet, is a Miami-based multidisciplinary artist, curator, and author of eleven poetry and prose collections. Born in Manhattan to Honduran immigrant parents, his work explores themes of family, memory, and legacy. His typewriter poetry was recently featured on Bravo's The Real Housewives of Miami, and he currently serves as poet-in-residence at 1 Hotel South Beach. Fuentes is promoting Poetry City, a new collection inspired by the rhythms and stories of Miami. In 2023, he received the inaugural Miami-Dade Mayoral Poetry Commendation. He is recognized for his distinctive persona, driving a 1974 Dodge Dart with a trunk full of vintage typewriters and wearing typewriter ribbon for a mustache.